Infinite Sight

Barbara Custer

Night to Dawn

Night to Dawn Magazine & Books LLC
P. O. Box 643
Abington, PA 19001
www.bloodredshadow.com
ISBN: 978-1-937769-42-0
Copyright by Barbara Custer 2015

Illustrator: Marge Simon
Editor: Gemini Wordsmiths

As always, to Michael, a survivor in his own right.

****

I would like to thank my beta readers at the Hatboro Writers' Group for their input and support; also, a big thank you goes out to Ann Stolinsky and Ruth Littner of Gemini Wordsmiths for their patience and good humor when helping me through the edits.

Table of Contents

Chapter One
Baby Miller's Death

When Lilly disconnected the tubing from Baby Miller's ventilator, shrill alarms announced his plummeting oxygen saturation and impending cardiac arrest. Born 14 weeks before his due date, Baby Miller tottered between life and death during his short life. Loud noises agitated him and stress caused his oxygen readings to drop. Lilly had unhooked his tubing to put a breathing treatment into the line, never realizing that disconnecting any tubing on his type of ventilator triggered a shutdown operation.

She pushed the "reset" button. *Surely, that will enable his machine to deliver breaths again.* Instead, the ventilator whistled harsh, accusatory notes and Baby Miller's oxygen saturation took a nosedive; she now knew that the tiniest error could send him into oblivion. A respiratory therapist who specialized in adult care, Lilly knew little about premature infants and the equipment that kept them alive.

She scanned the dials, hoping to find a hint

of what she could do to fix the problem, but the dim overhead lights made it impossible for her to make out the tiny numbers and symbols on Miller's ventilator control panel. As she two-fingered her cellphone from her scrub pocket, about to call a coworker for help, the argument she had earlier with her supervisor flashed through her mind.

"Diane, please send a pediatric therapist to the Neonatal Intensive Care Unit. I don't feel I have enough training to work with babies or their ventilators."

Lilly gazed at the other therapists, her eyes vulnerable, pleading for help. Instead of assisting her, the others kept quiet and listened with wide-eyed fascination.

"I don't have an extra therapist," Diane told her. *"Chadwick has assigned you the NICU rotation this week, so you'd better make yourself comfortable."*

Why me?

Months before, Chadwick had circulated a memo offering his staff an optional seminar on the NICU's new ventilators. Beside her name, Lilly had checked off "Not interested." Most of the data involving premature infants sounded like Greek and the small print didn't help. A note from her doctor explained her vision problems, and the ensuing discussion between her and management wound up on the slippery slope of what she could and couldn't do. Despite the note and her protests, Chadwick had ordered her to attend the seminar.

"Do something!"

Lilly jerked her body sideways, dropping her cellphone. Baby's Miller mother, a reed-thin woman in cashmere who towered over Lilly, jerked her thumb toward Baby Miller's heart monitor. The ventilator emitted harsh, accusatory notes, and each note sent chills up Lilly's spine. After calling a code, the boy's nurse fed him oxygen through his nose from a plastic bag. His oxygen readings continued to drop.

"Idiot!" the mother shouted at her. "You turned off my baby's ventilator!"

"No, I didn't." Lilly drew in her breath, wincing at a bolt of pain that knifed through her stomach. It wasn't the first time stress had made her ulcer active.

"I'm giving him one hundred percent oxygen, Missus Miller," a nurse beside them said. "The doctors are on their way here. Let's give Lilly room so she can check his ventilator."

The ventilator continued shrieking. A flood of shivers twisted Lilly's body; her mouth went dry. Why didn't the "reset" button work? She started toward the utility room to get a replacement ventilator until the alarm on Miller's cardiac monitor tolled. Miller's oxygen bottomed in the sixties, and the line on his cardiac monitor went flat. The doctor rushed to the crib side to give Miller chest compressions. Despite the code team's best effort, Miller's tiny body turned dusky. His heart remained deathly still.

"My baby!" His mother burst into a spate of

weeping. "You killed my boy!"

What can I say? That management had forced me to work in the NICU? Apologies and explanations sounded lame.

"Get out!" Miller's mother screamed. "Get out of here!"

Razor blades sliced through Lilly's stomach. The white heat of agony hurt so badly she could only stagger. The mother's shouts and accusations trailed behind her as she lurched toward the restroom in a sidestroke motion. She never made it. Vomit tasting like copper ripped through her throat, splashing onto the linoleum floor.

People in white lab coats rushed after her, calling her name. Too late. Lilly pitched headlong, hitting her head against the wall, clutching her gut, blood jetting from her mouth. Black dots rose before her eyes. Moments later, darkness waded in.

Chapter Two
A New Power

Lilly dressed for her walk, following the same route she'd taken daily since her release from the hospital, ten weeks after Baby Miller's death. The fall had gifted her with a concussion. Her stomach ulcer had perforated and bled, necessitating emergency surgery and a hiatus from work. At first the headaches had been brutal. Her abdominal incision burned like blazing charcoal in her gut and she could only walk as far as her driveway. Now the headaches and incision pain were gone, and she walked to the woods and back, covering over a mile. She'd go back to work in another week.

Lilly made a mental note to thank Muni and her other coworkers for informing Diane that they'd overheard Lilly's warning about her limited experience with the NICU's ventilator. Without their support, Lilly might have lost her job and her license. Instead, Diane assured her that her job remained intact, even after Miller's mother filed a lawsuit.

But her fall left repercussions. Since her fainting episode in the NICU, she became aware that she could read people's thoughts the same way someone might look through photographs or listen to a conversation. When her husband, Wade, demanded to know why, the doctors pointed to a CT scan image of her brain. It revealed bruising around the Broca and Wernicke's areas, the portions that influenced speech and comprehension. Her husband and the neurologist spoke in hushed tones—as if that would stop Lilly from reading their thoughts.

What are you saying, Doctor? Does she have a brain tumor?

No tumor, no lesions. Her neurological changes may have disturbed parts of her brain that had previously lain dormant. The changes are only transient.

At the hospital and later at home, Wade stayed up nights pacing, when he thought Lilly was asleep. Nightmares about her gift and the surgery troubled him, and he feared legal complications from her mishap with Miller. Sometimes he searched the Internet for information about potential lawyers, just in case.

Lilly never forgot the day Miller's lawyers showed up at her bedside. Three of them sat, facing her bed, questioning her about the mishap, her duties, and her training. Wade was there, too—he seldom left her bedside unless he had work or errands that couldn't wait. He remained silent, in a chair by the window, crossing and uncrossing his legs, then coming over to Lilly's bed to hold her hand.

Despite the painkillers, stabbing pain ripped

through her abdomen with any movement. Her head ached terribly and the lawyer's voices seemed to her like shouting. She answered their questions between gritted teeth. After she repositioned herself, the pain eased and she found herself scrutinizing their minds. She made out distorted images of Chadwick

After they left, she turned toward Wade and smiled. "I'm not in any trouble, honey. The lawyers need my story to confirm what other people said. They're going after Chadwick."

Wade shook his head, trembling. "They didn't say anything about Chadwick."

"No, but their thoughts about Chadwick came through loud and clear."

"If you have it right, this knack of yours could save us a lot of worry." Wade blotted his forehead with a tissue. "What about your biopsy? Were you able to get any read as to why your ulcer never got better?"

"No."

Lilly averted her eyes, not caring to admit that she'd sensed undercurrents of doom when she focused on her doctors. Ulcers that didn't heal could spell cancer, a disease which had ravaged her mother's lungs and blood cells before killing her. The word "cancer" appeared in her mind as a sign painted in bold red letters. Worst of all, the word floated in her surgeon's mind, ugly and as frightening as a grinning skull. During each examination, she shuddered under the blankets, expecting the word to roll off his tongue, making the possibility real.

At home, Lilly continued hearing others' thoughts. Like a beat of simple music, the central thought formed the basis of more complex thoughts. They usually came to Lilly in words or images. Her doctor's "cancer thoughts" centered around pictures of a shadow on her stomach X-rays. Wade's "cancer thoughts" flashed crimson with veins of pitch black.

Weeks later, the pathology report failed to show malignancy, and the doctors declared Lilly fit to work.

****

Wade, also a respiratory therapist, was working at Cherrydale Hospital tonight, 15 miles from their northeast Philadelphia home. He wasn't thinking about Lilly's operation. He was thinking about … about … and then commotion outside distracted her.

Lilly glanced out the window and gasped. The setting March sun usually colored the sky lavender; instead, rainbow lights flitted across her lawn and the surrounding houses. After donning her quilted jacket, she rushed outside and gazed skyward.

A circular object floated over the treetops, beaming blue, orange, and red rays to the earth. Covered with Gothic designs, it resembled a glittering Christmas ornament. The lights faded, and a boom followed. Blue fire engulfed the craft, and it fell from the sky. A deafening crash like shattering glass and crumbling metal echoed through the woods.

Chapter Three
UFO Crash Landing

The passengers on board must have sustained serious injuries. Who can I call for help? Did any of the neighbors hear the crash? In any case, the police would ask for addresses and cross-streets and she couldn't pinpoint where the crash happened. *I can't call Wade; he has another hour to go before he gives his end-of-shift report.*

What makes you think you can handle this yourself? With all your challenges – your thick bifocals, poor night vision, dietary restrictions to accommodate your reconstructed stomach - and now, this ability to pluck thoughts from people's minds. ... So until tonight, Lilly avoided the woods and anything else seemingly complicated, leaving those things for Wade to handle.

Wade couldn't help her this time.

Concern for any passengers nagged at Lilly, and she hurried back into the kitchen. She rooted through her purse for a flashlight and her cellphone. Outside again, squinting through her thick glasses, she gagged on the sulfuric stink of smoke wafting from the woods. Her sneakers thudded on the pavement; her light cast bright circles on the street. Vision problems notwithstanding, Lilly hied to the woods. Someone was in trouble.

In the woods, she coughed her way through a maze of twisted oaks. She hacked and gagged on the stink of sulfur; the smell was worse around the ship, which lay between shattered aisles of trees it had destroyed in its descent. Flames flickered from its open hatchway. The ship itself lay canted to one side with air bubbles bursting all around it. On its left side, pieces of metal scattered in the grass. Shining her light on the ship, Lilly happened upon warped metal strips protruding over one side. Underneath the ship, glowing embers leaped and twirled in a blue fiery dance. Face dripping with sweat, she shot glances right and left. *Where are the firemen? The police? My neighbors? Enormous Christmas ornaments like this don't crash and burn every day. Surely either radar or other scanner devices had detected this.*

Leaves crunched to her right, followed by a scraping of branches. Lilly charged into the brush, panting gasps escaping her lips. Her flashlight played over the grass and bushes, for without her light, she couldn't see to navigate in the dark. Her foot tapped against something—a shiny metal helmet rolled under a shrub. The branches separated. Lilly looked in and screamed.

A gloved hand reached for the helmet. The owner of that hand stepped from its hiding place, put its helmet on, and stared at Lilly with glowing red eyes. Dressed in a lime green spacesuit, it stood about her height. Its bald head, thin lips, and masculine features made it look like a male human, but the pointed ears and flattened nose with nostrils like tiny slits defined him as extraterrestrial. His jagged teeth chattered. He trembled like an electrified wire.

Lilly screamed again. "Get out of here," she shouted. "Go home!"

"I can't," the stranger said in perfect English. "My ship is ruined. I survived because I beamed myself to Earth before the main explosion." He huddled against the branches, teeth clicking, gloved hands outstretched in a supplicating gesture. "I'm running low on oxygen."

"Oh, Lord!" Lilly backed into a tree, rubbing her arms and shivering. "This can't be real."

"Of course I'm real." And as if to prove his point, the visitor grasped her hands.

Lilly recoiled, screaming again, and wrenched her hands free. "Please. Go. Away."

"I'm not going to hurt you." His voice took on a pleading tone. "You know how to provide oxygen. Please help me."

Why would this alien need oxygen, unless he requires a habitat that provides more oxygen than the earth —?

"My people require an atmosphere with forty percent oxygen to survive," he said, as if reading her thoughts. "My oxygen supply will last two hours, your time."

Lilly stared at the visitor, her hands pressed

against her trembling lips. A board on his chest flared red foreign symbols. Tubes led from the board to his helmet and backpack. Something bulged at his waist under a metallic band. *A gun, perhaps? Where is his parachute? How did he learn English?* Images surged from his mind, and then a complete picture floated above the babble of words and colors that she normally got from strangers. She saw the visitor marching through a grayish swamp with others dressed in steel-gray armor. He fired a plasma gun at someone in blue, killing him. Robed figures converged upon him, leading him into a room with slate walls. His companions' angry shouts warned that shit of some sort had hit the fan, forcing the alien's exile from his home.

Lilly's brow wrinkled as she continued studying him, still shaking. He wrapped his arms across his chest, shivering, and his jaw clinched, lips set in a grim line. *Perhaps his planet had gone to war, and his peers held him responsible.* "Who are you?" she asked at last.

"Laylok," he said. "I live on Eurosta, three million light years from your home. I've studied Earth through the years and learned English. Like you, we have our wars. An army of terrorists are trying to overthrow our rulers. We call these terrorists *giestan*, our word for hostile stranger. One of our soldiers wore the *giestan* uniform as a decoy. When my army attacked the *giestan*, my weapon felled the soldier. I had close friends among my peers who stood behind me, but the King sentenced me to slave labor, and eventually death by slow starvation and exposure in an extermination camp."

"So you came here to hide."

"No." The words came out clipped because of his chattering teeth. "Before the fuel tanks exploded, the King's officers were escorting me to this camp. The first explosion caused a power failure, destroying the electronic barrier, which unlocked my cell. The second blasted the fuel tanks. Since my cell was furthest from those tanks, I was able to escape and beam myself to Earth."

"You must feel terrified," Lilly said, thinking about the infant Miller and the way he'd suffered before he died. "Rest assured that I don't have any contact with Eurosta."

"That's unfortunate." He frowned. "Ships moving prisoners travel in pairs and our captain alerted the other ship about his ship's engine malfunction. I must contact my friends for help before the second crew realizes that I'm alive."

"Earth is a big planet, so no one will find you here, right?"

Laylok shook his head. "All soldiers have implanted tracking devices, so anyone who lands here can trace my location."

Lilly sighed. "I see."

"You seem like a kind person," Laylok said. "I'm shaking because the heating module in my suit has stopped working. I require temperatures about one hundred and fifty degrees Fahrenheit, so I crawled under your shrubs to get warm."

"The shrubs won't help," Lilly told him. "It's thirty degrees Fahrenheit."

"I guess ... I realized that." His shivering worsened. "I'm going to die soon unless you can help me get to a warm place."

In other words, he was going to freeze to death unless the officers from the twin ship caught him first. Maybe he's carrying lethal microbes. The people searching for him are no doubt vicious and do not forgive mistakes. Then Lilly thought about the Miller child again. *I wonder if Laylok has relatives. I can't let him die like I let Baby Miller die.*

"No way," she said. "God sent you to me so I could have a second chance."

"No god sent me," Laylok said in a reasonable voice. "The King's officers did. They punish the kind of mistake I made by execution."

"I've got an oxygen concentrator at home which can give you forty percent oxygen. My mother used oxygen before she died last fall and I never returned the equipment." She managed a smile. "Please call me Lilly. I'll do what I can –"

Another explosion interrupted her, hammering her to the ground and tossing the alien shuttle skyward like a toy. Shrapnel flew, and the smoke darkened the moon, giving it a blood red glow, almost the color of a total lunar eclipse. Above the roar, she heard a scream.

Kneeling behind the brush, she made out people, possibly police officers, dressed in dark uniforms. Their lights swept right and left, cutting paths in the grass and shrub. One officer pointed his light at Laylok's ship, which now lay in three pieces. *Perhaps these men are government agents.*

She imagined them seizing Laylok and torturing him by invasive experiments. If they spotted her, she could tell them she'd gone for a walk.

Oh, yeah? A voice piped up in her mind. *They'd ask why you're walking alone this time of night near a crash site.*

"Don't see anyone," the man nearest the ship said. "No one survived this."

"I've got a gut feeling we're being watched." His companion swept his light through the trees and brush again. "But by whom?"

By someone getting a second chance. Lilly gazed at the smoldering embers. She promised herself never to betray Laylok or report him to any authority. *Let the agents come and bust my kneecaps.*

While the men shone their lights, something slithered under the ship's crumbled hatchway. A lizard – at least it looked like one – with shiny red plates reared up and bit the officer nearest the ship on the leg. The officer shrieked. The lizard-like thing clung to his pant leg. Lilly gaped, frozen, at the creature's amber eyes. Its mouth chewed and swallowed. Blood spurted on the grass.

"Jesus, help me! HELP!" the young man shouted.

Chapter Four
A Reptile Called Death

The other officer fired at the creature, his shot sounding like the crack of a whip. The reptile did not budge. Another shot. The reptile continued feeding on the stricken man. The helpless man's cries grew weak. His partner bolted, screaming something into his cellphone.

Leaves rustled behind Lilly. Whirling around, she faced Laylok, arm extended, his hand brandishing a device shaped like a beeper. Yellow rays blazed at the reptile, consuming it in flames. The armed officer shifted his gaze toward them.

Lilly gulped, her throat dry. *I didn't see that.* Aloud, she said, "Laylok, we have to help that man."

"We can't. Poison from such creatures kills within minutes, and I don't have the antidote for it. I shot it because it was coming our way."

"Yeah ... well, we'd better run before his partner realizes who killed the beast. We're going to my house until we figure this out. Follow me and don't make a sound."

With that, Lilly tore off toward her house on

Thorndale Street. Laylok kept close behind her. Moments later, she cut a right on her street. Ahead, flashing lights cut reddish paths across the road. A police car coming from the opposite direction slowed to a stop by her house. Lilly swerved to her right up a gravelly road, past a cyclone fence that ran perpendicular to Thorndale Street. Her sneaker-clad feet swished through the damp grass, in concert with the clopping of Laylok's boots. Her auburn hair blew against her face but her mind spun at the sight of the fences blocking each yard, and the cars in driveways. Above, the reddish moon glowed against the dusky sky.

Moonlit shadows washed through the trees' branches. Lilly continued running, hidden from the police, sensed only by squealing birds that darted and dove. A stitch crept up her side, but she kept moving.

"My house is there." Gasping, she pointed toward a brick rancher. "The one with the blue car."

Using tree branches for support, Lilly scrambled over the picket fence surrounding her backyard. Laylok kept close. Then … voices. Wade was talking with a police officer.

"She's five-six," Wade said. "Caucasian with green eyes, bifocals, and shoulder-length red hair. She wears a quilted green coat. She's gotten hurt somewhere, has poor night vision, and hardly ever thinks to charge her cellphone. I tried to call her, got one ring, and it went straight to voicemail."

"Maybe she lost track of time?" the officer offered.

Lilly heaved a sigh. "Laylok," she whispered, "my husband, Wade, is speaking with a police officer, so I'm taking you in through the basement. I've got the concentrator there anyway, so I'll set it up and get you some blankets. Meantime, I'd like to know what happened back in those woods."

"Twenty-five *hydrii* were on board to guard my cell. The soldiers locked me and the hydrii in a section away from the rest of the craft so that these reptiles couldn't harm others. This way, they couldn't bite the soldiers. The hydrii's red metal cells enable them to survive extraordinary conditions, including crash landings. They look like a cross-breed between a snake and iguana, with sharp claws that give them mobility and a means to kill. Some hydrii grow six meters long. Their bite unleashes deadly poison the way it did when the *hydrus* attacked your officer." Laylok paused, giving Lilly a subtle glance. "One hydrus, twenty-five hydrii."

"I understand … more than I'd like." Cold fingers of dread inched up Lilly's neck, causing the hairs there to stiffen. "I'd better explain your predicament to my husband, Wade."

"Look …" Laylok's lip trembled. "I don't want to cause trouble. Your husband may not allow me to stay."

"He will if I ask him real nice," she said, smiling. Motioning Laylok to follow, she led him down the outside cement steps toward a padlocked door.

Inside, she guided Laylok through her paneled basement. A washer, dryer, and heater peeped from behind wooden steps that led to the kitchen upstairs. "Bathroom there," she said, pointing to a closet-sized room on her right. "The sink provides drinkable water ... assuming you can drink Earth water."

"I can."

"If you require sleep, you've got a makeshift bed." She waved her hand toward a sofa in the corner. "Would that work?"

"For my stay here, yes. At home, I don't require sleep as humans know it because we use a wireless, negative-cycle technology that renews our energy. Since I don't have access to this technology now, I appreciate the comfort."

Lilly smiled. "Then please sit. I'll rustle up the concentrator."

"Concentrator?" Laylok's brows arched slightly.

"Oxygen concentrator. It draws the gas from the atmosphere and pipes it through an oxygen device, such as a face mask or nasal prongs."

Laylok nodded and eased himself into the cushions while she rooted through the closet. The concentrator remained where she'd left it, along with nasal prongs, and a backup generator for emergencies. She rolled the concentrator to the sofa, plugged it in, and flipped the switch. The machine purred to life. "At six liters, the concentrator should give you forty percent," she said, adjusting the setting. She threaded the tubing to the oxygen port. "You'll have to take off your helmet."

Laylok snapped open his helmet visor and Lilly gagged on the stink of oil. Her fingers brushed his cheeks as she wedged the oxygen tubing around his chin and ears so that its prongs fit into his nostrils. His skin felt chilled like ice. She then draped a blanket over his head and around his shoulders. "I hope this works until I get more blankets. Do you have frostbite?"

"We don't get frostbite. Intense cold slows the heartbeat until it stops. The cold turns our skin dark gray and the heart can't pump oxygen. Intense cold can be fatal for my people within an hour, so I need those blankets."

"No problem." Lilly walked toward the staircase, turned, and rubbed her forehead. She sensed that Laylok meant well, but his thoughts, red intertwined with black, told her he was dreading a visit from the twin ship. "What about food? Can you eat what humans eat?"

"I eat proteins and complex carbohydrates. My body can't metabolize fatty foods, chemicals, or sugars."

Lilly leaned against the staircase, fighting an onslaught of dizziness. She squeezed her eyes shut. Images of red sharp-toothed reptiles leaping from violet shrubbery floated under her lids. The dizziness passed. "One last thing," she said. "How many of those hydrii survived the crash?"

"I don't know," Laylok said, lowering his eyes.

****

In the living room, a woman in a gray uniform looked up and smiled. *Not a police officer after all, but a Federal agent.* "Is this our missing person?" She folded her notebook and slipped it into her pants pocket. "Your husband was worried about you."

"I'm alright." Lilly smiled, reassuring herself. "I was just out for a walk."

"You've been gone at least two hours," Wade said after the agent left. His face shone with sweat, and, Lilly suspected, tears. "The news mentioned an explosion and something about a reptile attacking an officer. Right there in our woods, Lilly. What if you'd gotten hurt? It's damned serious. I called the police, but it's out of their hands, so they notified the Feds."

"I'm sorry you felt you had to do that." Lilly hugged him. "I'm OK. And I love you for worrying about me."

"The officer in question died," Wade continued in a strained voice. "You hate going out at night alone, and you've never gone near those woods. What got into you?"

"I thought someone had gotten hurt." Lilly drew in her breath, and then cleared her throat. A foreboding rose in her heart. *Any animal driven by hunger wouldn't hesitate to attack.* She imagined the hydrii, glittering red in the moonlight, repeatedly biting and swallowing. The officer's bloodcurdling shrieks echoed through her mind. She could smell their rancid odor in her nostrils. There was *no* satisfying their appetite. "Please listen with an open mind."

Wade sat in the leather chair that faced the TV. "I'm listening."

"I heard the crash, so I went out to the woods to check. I found a survivor from the ship. He told me what happened and then I saw the reptile that attacked the officer."

Wade jumped to his feet and gasped. "You *what?*"

"It's got tiny claws and red plates. Its bite contains a lethal poison, so I'm not surprised that the officer died. Laylok calls it a hydrus."

The color drained from Wade's face, causing his freckles to stand out like raised dots. His bulging eyes conveyed utter terror. "Who's Laylok?" he demanded. "What were you doing with him?"

"I was treating his hypothermia." Lilly struggled to keep her voice calm as she described the accident and her encounter with Laylok, including his oxygen and temperature requirements. Wade began pacing the room, his jaw tightening, lips setting in a grim line. His eyes narrowed into slits as she talked.

"He ran low on oxygen and his suit's heating unit broke, so I brought him here," she finished quietly. "Right now he's in our basement, breathing on Mom's oxygen concentrator. I'm getting him blankets and supper."

Wade nodded. "Of course." He sounded calm, but his pace didn't slow. Lilly thought she heard barely controlled terror in his voice. "You can't let him starve or freeze."

Why the calm front? Lilly looked at Wade, and then she understood. It flashed inside her mind the way her surgeon's "cancer thoughts" did, after the operation. She stared at Wade with widening eyes.

"You're calling the agent who was just here," she whispered in stunned surprise. "If you do, you'll get Laylok killed."

"We have no choice," Wade protested in a trembling voice. "You don't know what kind of germs he's carrying, and your ESP won't change that."

"It's telepathy, not ESP. You think Laylok brought the hydrii here on purpose. He didn't. His government's officers were escorting him to an extermination camp, and they brought the hydrii to guard his cell." She let out a long, shuddering breath. "At least one of those reptiles survived the crash."

"What if his shipmates survived, too?" Desperation and panic bled into his voice. "They'll come here looking for him."

Ships moving prisoners travel in pairs. Lilly hugged herself, shivering. "Maybe. But Laylok knows how to kill the hydrii." Lilly looked Wade in the eye, fighting hard to keep the panic from her voice. "I have to help him. Baby Miller's eyes have followed me since his death, and I don't want another pair of eyes following me."

"Oh, Lilly," Wade groaned, covering his eyes. "That's emotional blackmail."

"I'll tell the Feds about the hydrii, but I don't want any government scientists experimenting on Laylok like some lab rat. He also wants to contact Eurosta, his home, but I don't think that's possible."

"I don't either." Wade stopped his pacing and blotted his forehead with a handkerchief. "I'd better meet this fellow."

Chapter Five
Lilly's Guest

"Proteins and complex carbohydrates." Lilly scanned the plastic-covered dishes in the refrigerator. She reached for a platter of flounder and potatoes. While the food heated, she searched the closet for blankets and heavy socks. She then proceeded to the basement with the tray. Wade followed her, carrying an armload of clothes. "This should agree with you," she said, setting the tray on a metal crate besides Laylok.

Laylok picked up his fork stared at it, then turned his eyes toward Lilly. "We use a device like this in our communication systems, and ..." He looked up at Wade and flinched. The fork dropped. Laylok stared at his host with widened fearful eyes.

"It's OK, Laylok. This is my husband, Wade ... Wade Ashton." Lilly glanced sideways at her husband who still wore his work clothes. "Ditch the lab coat, Wade. It frightens him."

Wade shed his lab coat and hung it over the stair post. His face reddened and he grimaced as if he'd swallowed a fishbone. "He can't stay here,

Lilly," he said. "We've got to tell the Feds."

"If we do, they'll assume the worst about Laylok and shoot him." Lilly pointed toward the Eurostan. "Go on, talk to him. He understands and speaks English."

"I don't like this, Laylok," Wade told him. "Lilly just recovered from major surgery and the doctors don't want her having any stress."

"I understand your concerns," Laylok assured him. "I've got two children back home who worry about me getting shot."

Wade dropped the blankets on the sofa like hot coals. "What do you want with Lilly?" he demanded, ignoring Laylok's statement.

"Lilly graciously offered me oxygen and heavy clothing." Laylok gave Wade a pleading look. "Without those things, I will die. I also want to build a radio so I can contact my officers. I'm sorry for causing you trouble."

"You're the sorriest man I ever met," Wade muttered.

"That wasn't necessary, Wade." Lilly wrapped the blankets around Laylok's head, shoulders, and legs. "Laylok, relax and eat."

"How do you make your living?" Wade asked, giving Laylok a restless smile.

"You mean my function?" Laylok set down his fork and looked up at Wade. "I head the Cybernetic Resources Division, meaning I design robots and communication systems. Before the King sent me to war, I had no military training, and I explained this to him. He taught me how to use bombs, lasers, and chemical weapons, but not about tactical maneuvers. His foot soldier went to the *giestan* camp, wearing their blue uniforms, and I shot him by mistake."

"My God!" Lilly wiped perspiration from her forehead. "Something like that happened to me before I got sick, a mishap involving an infant's ventilator. I warned my superiors that I didn't feel confident working with sick babies, and that I needed more training, but no one listened. Something I did loused up the ventilator, and the infant died. So Wade and I understand what you're feeling." She gave her husband a hug and squeezed his hand. "Right, darling?"

"If you say so." Wade dragged his trembling fingers through his wavy brown hair. "I'm worried about those hydruses."

"Hydrii," Lilly corrected him. "One hydrus, two hydrii."

"Whatever." Wade fixed his gaze on Laylok. "I'll let you stay, my silence guaranteed, under two conditions. Lilly's safety comes first."

"I agree," Laylok said, picking up the flounder with his fingers. He swallowed it in one gulp, and then looked up at Wade again. "And your second?"

"Find out if any other hydrii survived and kill them. I assume you have the proper weapons."

"My guards confiscated my weapons, but I grabbed what I could carry before beaming myself. If we need more, I may be able to find them near the remains of the ship." Laylok reached into his holster and produced four beeper-like devices, each studded with a red, white, and green button. "These lasers contain certain chemicals that kill the hydrii."

"You can't chase those monsters with an oxygen concentrator and blankets." Lilly looked down at Laylok and rested her hand on his shoulder. "Can you teach us how to use these weapons?"

"I see no other way," Laylok said. "Fifty hydrii guarded my cell, and I don't know how many survived. They want fresh meat and your guns won't kill them." Another swallow, followed by a glance. Eyes back on Wade. "You just ..."

"Leave Lilly out of this," Wade cut in. "She never handled firearms and she can't see well at night."

"So what happens if one attacks me at night and I'm alone?" questioned Lilly. "Assuming I can see that ... that *thing*, I'll trip over my heels trying to escape."

"Don't go anywhere without a flashlight," Laylok advised her. "Your vision may not cause a problem anyway since you'll sense its approach with your mind."

Lilly swallowed hard. "What do you mean by that?"

"You're a telepath," Laylok told her. "I felt you reading me when we first met. I, too, can communicate by thought. All of my people do."

"It happened after my ... my surgery." She was going to say "...my concussion," but she didn't want Laylok to think she was brain damaged. "Afterward, people's minds became open books."

"Not surgery," Laylok said. "It happened after you fell and sustained a concussion."

Wade began to pace, but remained silent.

"Think something you'd like me to know." Laylok regarded Lilly with the intensity of a scientist studying a prized specimen. "Any thought will do; just think it hard. I want to see how strong your power is."

"Alright." Lilly considered this a moment, gathered her concentration, and then flung it out at Laylok. At the last instant, some instinctive part of her rose up and blunted the thought's raw force. Still, the thought whizzed forward like a flying saucer.

WELCOME TO EARTH, LAYLOK!!

Laylok winced and jerked back into the sofa cushions. His teeth came together with a hard click. Yellow blood ran from his lip in a thin trickle.

"Laylok!" Lilly cried with stunned horror. "What did I do?"

"I'm not sure." Laylok smiled. "Your ability would impress my people."

Wade paused by the staircase, shaking his head. "The doctors couldn't explain it, in any way that made sense. Will this ability enable her to defend herself?"

"It might." Holding his beeper-shaped device to the light, Laylok singled out each button. "Green activates the lasers. White stuns your enemy, and red will engulf it in flames."

Lilly took the weapon from Laylok. The feel of cold metal chilled her to the bone. "Maybe the hydrii will confine their hunting to the woods."

Wade shook his head. "I wouldn't bet on it."

****

Throughout the weekend, Lilly watched the news to find out if any more hydrii attacked after the crash. Saturday, three soldiers searched the woods, armed with tranquilizing darts, grenades, and carbines. They found their target ... six hydrii. The soldiers' gunfire struck them, but their darts and bullets bounced off the creatures' hard plates. The grenades missed their mark; the creatures slithered to the side. The soldiers retreated, but not quickly enough. The creatures' jaws closed around their legs, injecting the poison that would kill them in a few short hours.

Sunday morning, two officers in pressurized suits searched the woods. The reptiles' pointed teeth ripped through the Teflon suits as if they were fine tissue paper. Ditto casualties.

Sunday evening, thunderheads gathered in the sky, and by eight o'clock, rain came down in torrents. After laying out her work clothes, Lilly crawled into bed—alone, since Wade was working a double shift. The beeper device went under her pillow. She'd just drifted to sleep when Laylok's strangled cry jarred her awake.

"Lilly, help me! I can't breathe!"

Lilly bolted up, eyes open like window shades, but the room was quiet. Laylok's scream was coming from the deep recesses of her mind. She must have been asleep longer than she thought because Wade lay beside her, breathing deep, rhythmic respirations. With shaky fingers, she clicked on her lamp. No light.

She felt eyes following her every movement, watching, waiting.

Lilly eased from the covers and groped toward her bureau where she'd returned the flashlight. After slipping into a robe, she stared out the night-blackened window. The power failure blanketed the streets in darkness. As she brandished her light outside, a hideous lizard reared its head, fangs gleaming, claws scraping against the bricks of the house.

I imagined that. The wind's making the tree branches scrape against the house.

Lilly exhaled a whisper of fear when she realized that the power blackout had cut Laylok's oxygen supply. She'd have to run to the basement and set up the generator.

Very simple. Go to the basement. Hook the oxygen concentrator to the generator. Turn on the generator. Easy to do since it runs on a battery. Come back upstairs. I did this enough times when I cared for Mom.

Oh, yes, and don't faint if a hydrus gets into the basement.

She slipped the beeper weapon into her robe pocket and walked to the hallway, trying to shake the mantle of fear that shrouded her. The idea of leaving Wade alone left her with a sick feeling, though she couldn't say why. She made her way to the living room, playing her light. Everything in it appeared undisturbed.

See? No monsters here.

She hesitated at the basement door, not wanting to go downstairs, but Laylok needed a functional concentrator. The lack of oxygen would stress his heart.

Remember Baby Miller.

But the hydrii...

What hydrii? You merely heard branches scraping against the house.

"The hell I did."

The sound of her own voice made Lilly jump, but the dead certainty in it made her move forward. She retrieved her firearm, holding it perpendicular to the floor; its buttons cast rainbow shadows against the hardwood floor. Her slippers whispered toward the door. Her nerves sang like wires. She thrust the door open and shone her light. Her mind stiffened for whatever was lying in wait.

"Lilly?" Laylok cried in a gasping voice when he heard the basement door open. "I'm not getting any air."

"We had a power failure." Swallowing hard, she forced calmness into her voice. "Don't worry. I've got an emergency generator."

She put her hand on the wooden banister. Thirteen steps stretched ahead of her; she counted them enough times to know. *Thirteen wooden steps and no hydrii crawling on any of them. Of course not.* She and Wade installed steel-framed windows and doors when they'd bought the house.

The self-assurance did little to quiet her trembling. The house, so dark and full of shadows even with her flashlight, made it necessary to navigate by touch. That, and her poverty of night vision. Her pulse thudded in her throat. *Keep moving,* her mind screamed, *before your friend dies like Baby Miller.*

At that thought, Lilly skittered down the steps. Her flashlight cast bright circles on Laylok's white face and his gasping respiration discouraged further delay. Yet, slithering noises from outside held her attention.

The rain, of course. It poured with a vengeance.

Lilly paused before the shelves, trying to remember where she'd stored the generator. Shining her light, she spotted its gray siding on the bottom shelf. Using her weight as leverage, she pulled the generator onto the floor and rolled it toward the stairs, past the washer and dryer, to the sofa bed bathed in pools of shadow. On legs stilted with fear, she turned left, ready to set the generator by the oxygen concentrator. Then a draft caressed her calves. She turned toward the door, already knowing she was in trouble. Hissing issued from a crack in the door base.

Not a crack, but a widening, jagged hole. How could something chew through steel?

A hydrus gnawed on the opening, squeezed through, and was charging at her. Its yellow eyes lit with a murderous glow, illuminating the sharp teeth layering its mouth. The hydrus whistled across the cement floor. Lilly jumped sideways and barked her hip against the staircase.

"Lilly, the gun!" Laylok croaked.

Lilly jammed her fist into her pocket. Empty. Her weapon lay on the floor by the washer. *I must have dropped it while I was hauling the generator.* Clicking and rattling sounded behind her but that seemed so far away and unimportant. A monster had broken into her basement. It paused, as if trying to choose between her and Laylok; then it came at her with deadly speed. Instinctively she leapt over the steps, seconds before the hydrus buried its teeth into a wooden riser.

The hydrus hissed and writhed, trying to free its mouth. Its plated tale wricked under the staircase, its plates crackling like popcorn popping. The tail snagged Lilly by the ankle, causing her to sprawl onto her stomach. Only dimly aware of movement at the sofa, she screamed, her right leg submerged in an ocean of agony. Her hands flailed, groping for the beeper-shaped weapon – then she saw it, just two inches ahead of her fingertips. Tail curled around her leg, the hydrus dragged her along the floor, away from her firearm and under the staircase. Its mouth pulled away from the riser with a sickening crunch. Lilly screamed, bracing herself for an agonizing death.

Chapter Six
A Night of Terror

Rays flared through the room, engulfing the hydrus. The reptile squealed and released its grip on Lilly's ankle. Its head and trunk collapsed in a fiery haze, charred and reeking like spoiled meat. Moaning and shaking her head, Lilly pedaled with her feet, trying to shove herself toward the door. Laylok stood by the washer, panting, shoulders shivering under the blankets. His right hand held a beeper device from which red smoke wafted. Lilly continued pedaling with her feet. One slipper came off and landed on its side. Pain sank into her calf with each movement. A thin stream of blood trickled down her leg, for the plates from the hydrus had lacerated her skin. The pedaling stopped. She leaned against the wall, gagging on the stink of oil and smoke, listening to the crackling flames, watching the hydrus. Its plates melted and ran together, oozing yellow pus.

Footfalls thumped from the kitchen upstairs. The basement door banged open. Wade sprinted down the steps in his pajamas, wielding a fire extinguisher. Somewhere from an upper room, the smoke alarm blared throughout the house. Wade pulled the pin on the fire extinguisher as he aimed the nozzle toward the base of the fire.

Shrill alarms from outside harmonized with the smoke alarms in the house. Lilly was back in the NICU, staring at Baby Miller. Something went wrong with his ventilator and the alarm on its front panel whistled louder and louder.

Miller's mother materialized from nowhere, dressed in her cashmere outfit. "Idiot!" she screamed. "You turned off my baby's ventilator."

"No, I didn't," Lilly whimpered. Her groping hands fumbled for the machine's "reset" button. The whistling intensified. Baby Miller's face turned blue and the buzzing monitors announced his cardiac arrest. Strong hands grabbed her shoulders.

"Please don't yell at me." She shrunk against the wall, arms wrapped around herself, head bowed. "I'm sorry."

"No one's yelling at you." Wade's gentle voice invaded her consciousness. "I heard a ruckus in the basement, so I called the police."

Lilly rubbed her eyes. Wade cradled her close, rubbing her shoulder. Images of the NICU and Baby Miller's ventilator faded, replaced by that of her familiar basement furniture. The fire died, leaving the reptile's blackened skull and plates in a pool of yellow liquid. Two firefighters stood in the doorway whispering in hushed tones, but Lilly's eyes roved through the basement, searching for Laylok. *Oh my God, he left without his oxygen!*

"You were thinking about the NICU, and ... holy shit!" Wade shone his light on Lilly's blood-stained foot. "Did that thing bite you?"

Lilly shook her head. "Its tail caught me and cut me." Her breath hitched. "No hospital, no doctors, please. They'll want to know ..."

"Sh-h-h!" Wade held his finger to his lips and then draped a blanket over her shoulders. "The Feds are here. Let's see if you can walk and if so, go outside."

"Laylok needs his oxygen."

"I think our guest managed to fend for himself ... at least for the moment."

Lilly shot a glance toward Laylok's bed. Empty. His blankets were gone, too. The concentrator, nonfunctional without electricity, remained. Perhaps he was trying to get the power going somehow. She tried reading his thoughts, but her leg—oh, how it hurt! She hobbled to the door, moaning and shaking her head.

The outside steps loomed like Mount Everest. Lights from the agents' cars cast reddish shadows on the lawn and the windows. The rain stopped. "It doesn't look like you broke anything," Wade said, clasping his hand around her waist. "I've got a first aid kit in my car. Let's see about getting you bandaged."

Lilly hiked her gown and robe, revealing bruises the size of silver dollars on her right lower calf. While Wade dressed her wound with ointment and gauze, the agents searched her yard. Two of them, a man and a woman in pressurized suits, went into the house, carrying metal boxes. Moments later, they approached, eyes on Lilly.

"Mrs. Ashton, I'm Agent Kelly Garrison." The woman pointed to her companion. "My partner, Agent Garcia. Who ... or what ... killed that thing?"

"My Molotov cocktail," Wade said, looking up from his ministrations. "I soaked a napkin with oil and stuffed it into a glass. After I lit it with a match, I threw it at that creature."

Lilly watched the agents, furrowing her brows. Both of them smiled, but Garcia's eyes narrowed to crinkled slits, focusing on Wade.

That guy's feeding us a line of bull.

"He's telling the truth," she said. "I cut my leg on the glass."

"Oh." Garcia jerked his head toward Lilly. "I see."

Garrison turned toward her, frowning. "What's with the oxygen equipment?"

"The concentrator belonged to my mother." Lilly gazed toward the house, lips set in a grim line. *Laylok, where are you?*

I'm hiding in your garage, his voice whispered in her mind. *I'm using my own tank. It will last one more hour.*

"You ought to get that leg checked," Garcia said. "I'll call an ambulance."

"There's no need to do that. Wade already took care of me. It's just one open wound. The rest are bruises."

"The lab will do an autopsy on that alien," Garrison said. "I have other questions, but I'll ask them after I see the report."

Lilly studied Garrison, weighing her as a potential ally. *Ruddy complexion, light brown hair, rounded blue eyes. Thirty-year-old supporting her special needs brother and their mother, who had end-stage leukemia.* She might understand, badge notwithstanding, that sometimes the law involved gray areas, and then the words played through Lilly's mind: *Mrs. Ashton's hiding something.*

No surprise there. Garrison's job demanded questions that neither Lilly nor Wade wanted asked. "No problem," she said. "And please call me Lilly."

"Very well." Garrison smiled. "Steer clear of that basement until I get the report. And get that leg looked at right away."

****

"You covered for Laylok," Lilly said to Wade after the officers left. "Thank you."

"Despite his respiratory problems, he fired the shot that saved you." Wade heaved a long rattling sigh sounding like leaves blowing down the street. "I promised I'd look out for him if he put your safety first."

"Laylok's hiding behind the lawn mower." Lilly waved her hand toward the garage. "He's wearing his suit with an hour's worth of oxygen and he's probably half-frozen by now. The concentrator's useless without power and Garrison declared our basement off-limits anyway."

"I'll get him the blankets and put him up in our guestroom. Some of my Cherrydale Hospital buddies owe me favors and will help me get oxygen tanks or other equipment we can borrow until the power comes back on." Wade sighed again. "Honey, I don't know how long we can keep this quiet."

Grabbing Wade's hand, Lilly struggled to her feet. The cut stung, causing her to favor her left leg. "Give me a moment to dress," she said. "I'm coming with you."

"To haul oxygen equipment? You're hurting too much. Why didn't you ask me to help you with the generator?"

"You'd worked sixteen hours."

"I have all day to sleep tomorrow. You don't." With a grin, Wade laid his hands on her shoulders. "Humor me and go to bed. I'll keep your friend safe."

Lilly smiled, though her heart still thudded. "I appreciate it."

She hobbled up the porch steps and down the hall to the bedroom. She lay on her side, injured leg propped on a pillow. The house seemed full of a thousand slithering sounds – whispering, hissing, and rattling on the floor. A horrible understanding dawned, and Lilly knew what made the hydrii so dangerous: *Their keen intelligence enables them to remember people. What if they target my house?*

Chapter Seven
Hydrii Everywhere

When Lilly awoke, her leg throbbed as if sliced by shattered glass. She donned her pink scrubs and a lab coat, and tucked the laser weapon into her pants pocket. She then proceeded to the guest bedroom to check on Laylok. He had curled up under a mountain of blankets including the electric blanket. A new concentrator fed him oxygen.

In the kitchen, Wade brewed coffee. Shadows circled his blue eyes and his face bleached milk pale when he looked at Lilly. "You should've gone to a hospital," he said.

Lilly shifted her gaze toward the coffeepot, trying not to read his thoughts. It crossed her mind that a witty comeback about work and death might elicit a smile. On second thought, Wade's brows knitted together, a warning that he wasn't in a joking mood. Work was the last thing on his mind.

But then, what was funny about an infant dying, alien terrorists, or reptiles that killed with one bite? Lilly swallowed hard, fighting an onslaught of tears.

"Honey, they will only allow so much sick leave before my job goes up for grabs. Besides ..." Her voice cracked. Another gulp. "Besides, if the hydrus had poisoned me, I would've been dead by now."

"Instead, you lived to talk about it." Wade nodded, as if confirming this to himself. "Laylok assured me that only the saliva and blood contain toxins. I suspect these creatures singled us out because we're hiding a prisoner. This morning, when I went out to get the newspaper, one of those things came at me from behind a bush."

"Oh, no!" Lilly inhaled a sharp breath. "You didn't get ..."

"I shot him before he could bite. The officers who got killed were searching blindly, but killing hydrii is doable once you understand the beasts. Good thing, too, since we live and work so close to the woods. You're favoring your left leg, I see. Are you up to handling patients? And can you maneuver on your leg enough to shoot?"

"I hope so." Memories of last night's horror became so intense, so overwhelming, that Lilly grabbed her lab coat sleeves, and then pulled at her hair. In spite of her best efforts to put on her game face, salty tears spilled from her eyes and down her cheeks. "By bringing Laylok here, I led those monsters to our home. I'm sorry."

"No need to be," Wade said, and his arms surrounded her like a warm blanket. "The hydrii survived the crash and would have attacked our home anyway. Without Laylok, we'd have no way to defend ourselves. Remember that."

"He wants to contact his own officers."

"I know," Wade said in a low voice. "We don't have the means to contact Eurosta or any other planet. So I humored him and let him tinker with our computer."

****

In the respiratory therapy department at the hospital, Lilly peeked at the assignment roster and gasped, her heart thudding. Someone had scrawled her name inside the box labeled "NICU," and she found herself in the NICU ward. Baby Miller's ventilator flashed a "vent inoperative" sign, punctuated by shrill alarms.

"Do something!" Miller's mother shouted behind her.

"No-o-o-o!" Squeezing her eyes shut, Lilly massaged her forehead, hoping to blot out the memories. *I should've looked for job at a hospital that doesn't have a neonatal unit.*

Drawing in a deep breath, she darted another glance at the roster. She'd looked at the night shift schedule by mistake, and the NICU night therapist's name was Leila. With trembling fingers, Lilly snapped up the day shift roster besides it. Diane had assigned her to Two Tower, an adult noncritical care floor. She heaved a sigh of relief.

During the nightshift therapist's oral report, she scribbled out the diagnoses and treatment plans, nodding at the right times; but images of the hydrii continued to haunt her thoughts. She remembered the creature's tail cutting into her leg, its teeth ripping into her stairs. The pungent stench of its melting plates lingered in her nostrils.

Drawing in a deep breath, she looked across the table at Muni, who was writing up his assignment. He nodded and smiled encouragingly, but his widened eyes and the unspoken words behind them read, *she looks terrible. Why didn't they allow her more sick time?* Though Muni spoke with a thick Indian accent, his thoughts came through clearly.

Her eyes then shifted toward two other therapists getting and giving reports beside him. Their sharp eyes and thin-lipped frowns discouraged any conversation, but their minds became open books.

NICU again? Diane's going to hear about this.

One day, I'll quit without notice, and see how they like it.

"Lilly?" A woman's soft voice interrupted her thoughts.

With a gasp that echoed in her head, Lilly jerked herself out of the darkness. The two therapists whose thoughts she read continued with their reports. A blonde woman stood in the doorway, motioning to her. Diane, her supervisor.

"What happened to your leg?" Diane asked.

An iron lump rose in Lilly's throat, but she did not cry. Some coworkers liked to talk and a crying jag provided grist for malicious gossip. "Clumsy me," she said, forcing a laugh. "I dropped a lamp and cut myself on the broken glass."

"It looks painful." Diane's voice edged with worry. "You were limping when you clocked in. Are you going to be OK?"

"Sure." Lilly stepped further into the hall, meeting Diane's gaze and sensing genuine concern. "Sometimes I think about Baby Miller. I want a thorough orientation to the NICU ventilators before you assign me there again."

"I pulled you from the NICU roster after your mishap with Baby Miller. Chadwick already knows." Diane's voice softened. "Just relax and take care of that leg."

****

During the next three days, Lilly, Wade, and Laylok took turns guarding the house. Each time Lilly assumed her watch, any smile she attempted morphed into horror; her heart thudded *ka-boom, ka-boom, ka-boom.* A hydrus might chew through the walls or slither through a crack in the floorboards at any second. It never happened. Wade changed her bandage every morning and checked her wound for signs of infection or poisoning, but he found none.

During Thursday morning's shift report, Brian Chadwick, the department director, marched into the conference room, eyes narrowed, white lab coat flapping against his pant legs. He leaned against the bulletin board. "I heard some of you have exempted yourselves from working certain floors," he began, voice oozing with fury. "This is inappropriate and will not be tolerated."

Diane, who sat near the door sipping coffee, looked away, her face beet red. *I tried to reason with him.* Her thoughts come through as clear as printed text.

Lilly swayed, sank forward, and scribbled calculations on the back of her assignment sheet. The formulas came from Laylok's mind; he was using them to build a radio. The figures didn't make sense, but her hand scribbled away until she worked her way toward the end of the sheet.

"Lilly, put the pen down and listen," Chadwick ordered.

Lilly tried to, but waves of dizziness hit, making the room spin. Trying to clear her head, she looked at Muni, who sat beside her with his eyes on her sheet. "What's that?" he mouthed, pointing to her formulas.

Lilly grinned and shrugged. "No idea why I did that."

"I've never seen anything —"

"This whispering has to stop." Chadwick heaved an impatient sigh and fixed his gaze on Lilly. "Two people called out sick. Lilly, I'm assigning you to the NICU."

Lilly returned Chadwick's unrelenting stare. His gray eyes became flecks of ice, and images she'd gotten from Laylok played through her mind, enabling her to picture the Eurostan King's cold eyes when he sent Laylok into battle. "I'll need more training," she told him.

"No one has time to hold your hand. Do us all a favor and grow up."

Images rose before Lilly: Chadwick as a child, cringing from his father's razor strop and his threats. *Bri-baby! Do us all a favor and grow up.*

"Oh, my God!" The words tore from her mouth before she could stop them. "Your father called you 'Bri-baby.'"

The other therapists broke into raucous laughter. Chadwick's face turned purple; a vein throbbed across his forehead. "That's enough, Lilly," he warned.

So that's why he acts so mean. Lilly covered her eyes, trying to blot out the colors and words that assaulted her mind. It wasn't the first time she'd tuned into someone's past, and now, Chadwick's memories played through her mind in shades of deep red, purple, and blue intertwined in sickening patterns. "My God, you're repeating what your father said to you."

Muni folded his brown-skinned hands and looked at Chadwick. "Give Lilly my assignment," he offered. "I'll take the NICU."

Chadwick swerved toward Muni. In doing so, he knocked his fist against Diane's cup, spraying the table and Muni's assignment sheet with steaming coffee. He yanked Lilly by the shirtsleeve. "That did it," he shouted. "You're coming to the office."

The sudden movement jammed Lilly's injured leg against the chair. "Ow!" she cried, gripping the table to steady herself. "Let go of me."

Chadwick's asking for another lawsuit.

How did she come up with Bri-baby?

Hands gripping Lilly's arm, Chadwick marched her to his office, three doors from the conference room. Lilly sensed that he was headed for a breakdown, having endured a harsh father and hordes of temperamental employees. Images of him reaching for a rope with which to hang himself flashed through her mind. His parting thought jerked her out of his head with a gasp, for she sensed he wanted to hang her, but was fighting the urge. The thoughts came to her in black print letters emblazoned with gold.

"Sit down," he ordered in a voice reeking with contempt.

Lilly sat in a chair facing his desk, fists clenched, knuckles white. Her fear of Chadwick came flooding back, distracted only by the grating noises that came from the paneled wall facing the courtyard. In the next minute, dark tumors of rage blossomed, chasing away her fear. *Diggity damn! I have enough at home with the hydrii. Why am I letting myself be intimidated by an administrator who acts like an overgrown kid getting even for an imagined slight in the playground? And, speaking of Administration, who decided that the Respiratory Therapy Department should have first-floor offices? It had never mattered before, but now, it seems working anywhere on the first floor is like ringing the dinner bell for the hydrii.* At that idea, Lilly shivered. Her hand reached for the beeper-shaped weapon pressed against her thigh.

Chadwick's piercing gaze raked her with freezing contempt. "Who do you think you are, refusing an assignment as if it were some cafeteria entrée?"

Lilly gulped, her chest tightening. Those scratching sounds. No, not scratching. Rocks crumbling. "I'm not refusing anything. I'm asking for more training so I can avoid future mishaps like the one with Baby Miller. It takes longer for me to learn because I can't read the small print on the controls."

Chadwick leaned forward, his white-sleeved arms folded across his blotter, his gaze intent on Lilly. "Your mishap with Miller was unfortunate," he conceded. "So next time, pay attention. Use a magnifying glass if you have to."

"I have one, but I need more training with the neonatal ventilators."

"I don't have time to hold your hand," Chadwick said in a voice of deepest frost. "Consider this a verbal warning."

Splintering sounds punctuated his sentence, and a long section of plaster jumped from the baseboard and clattered to the side. Another crack followed the sound of something tearing through brick and mortar. A hydrus's squarish head, covered with crumbled rocks and debris, gnawed its way through the hole in the baseboard. It chewed and spat, sending metal fragments flying across Chadwick's office.

Lilly jumped to her feet and onto her chair, ignoring the stinging in her leg. "Chadwick, run!"

"This hysteria of yours is ... holy shit!" Chadwick's self-assured authoritarian look disappeared, and a scared-little-boy expression replaced it. "Call the police!"

With that, he bolted from his office, letting out fright-filled screams. Lilly steadied herself on the chair, keeping her eyes on the baseboard. The reptile's teeth crunched through the wall again, widening the hole, and then one claw appeared, seeking purchase on the beige rug. Its eyes gleamed yellow, and a horrible, grinning malignancy looked out at her.

Her hand jammed inside her pocket, fingers closing around the beeper gun. Teeth chattering, she aimed her weapon and fired just as the wall split. The hydrus charged toward the desk. Red rays hit the scales along the reptile's crest, just behind its head, causing its plates to explode into flames. The creature let out harsh squeals and skittered to the window.

Lilly stared at the floor, gauging her distance to the door. *Eight feet.* In three bounding steps, she made it to the hall. Her leg exploded into white hot agony with each step, drawing strangled cries from her lips. She slammed the door shut behind her seconds before something heavy crashed against it. Keeping her eyes on the door, she backed down the hall, closing doors as she went.

Hushed whispers caught her attention. Muni and Diane peeked out from the conference room. "What's going on?" asked Muni. "I saw Chadwick running like his pants had caught fire."

"His office caught fire. I think he's hiding ..." *in the restroom,* but she resisted the urge to say. *Hiding and snorting Jack Daniels.* Lilly trembled against the wall at the liquid terror drawing a thin line of ice up her spine, cresting at her shoulders. Even from where she stood, the thumping, tinkle of window glass, and crackling flames chilled her to the bone. Red smoke wafted from under the door. "He screamed at me to call the police."

"Why didn't he ... never mind, I'll call them." Diane's voice laced with panic. "Hurry up, close the oxygen valves before there's an explosion. I've got to evacuate this floor."

"I've got the oxygen." Muni sprinted toward the shutoff valve by the exit. "What started the fire?"

Before Lilly could answer, the door banged open, and three security guards burst into the hallway. "The police are on their way," one of them said. "What's this about a reptile?"

Oh, great. Lilly clutched her forehead. *Last thing we need are these rent-a-cops.* "The animal ... reptile chewed its way into Mr. Chadwick's office," she said through clenched teeth.

The officer's face paled. "Big thing with red plates and teeth?"

"Yes. I shot it but wound up setting the office on fire. Where are the ..." Lilly's voice trailed off as the officer yanked a fire extinguisher from the wall and ran toward the office. He cracked the door, screamed, and then bolted, the reptile in pursuit. As he passed Muni, he dumped the extinguisher into Muni's arms. He then tore off toward the exit, followed by the other officers.

Lilly leveled her arm again, and fired straight at the creature. This time, her shot bathed the entire creature in fire. More squealing, and then the creature went still. Muni doused the flames with the extinguisher, and then he moved to the office.

He cracked the door, nodded, and then walked back to Lilly.

"There's no fire, just smoldering." He panted. "I heard about this reptile on the news. You ought to see a doctor."

"I'm alright, but Mister Mighty Mouth's nonsense has to stop." With a deep sigh, Lilly knocked on the bathroom door. "Mr. Chadwick, the creature's dead. You can come out now."

Chadwick cracked the door, his eyes bulging, face ash-white. Dark amber liquid drooled down his chin. His breath reeked of liquor. "What happened back there?" he asked.

"I saved your life." Lilly met Chadwick's gaze, the fear gone from her voice. "I assume you watch the news and know what could have happened."

"What?" Chadwick wagged his head. He straightened his tie and lurched into the hall. "You assume right. So what do you want? A raise? Time off with pay?"

"No more NICU rotations. I want that written warning gone from my file, too."

"You think you got me by the short hairs, don't you?"

"It's not about power; it's about doing the right thing." Her trembling stopped. Her leg still ached, but her mind felt sharp and accurate. "You wouldn't want me filing an ADA complaint with the Department of Justice."

"I should fire you for carrying a concealed firearm, but you saved our lives and Muni's. So I'm giving you a clean slate." Chadwick dragged his quivering fingers through his silver hair. "I'd better see if my office is still standing."

Another officer emerged from the outer door leading to the stairwell; this one wore a hazmat suit. Lilly and Chadwick followed him to the office. The furniture appeared intact but the wall facing the courtyard was charred. Red crusty shells mixed with yellow pus streaked the floor in the office and hall, oozing smoke and an acrid stench.

"Someone from the lab should look at this," the officer said. "Who killed that thing?"

"Lilly." Chadwick gave a pompous grin. "Since you officers are too incompetent to do your job."

The stairwell doors opened again, followed by footsteps. "We can't do our job when a certain someone withholds information," said a female voice.

Lilly whirled around and gasped. Agent Garrison stepped closer and faced her, flanked by two men also wearing hazmat suits.

"Those things seem to follow you," Garrison observed in a dry voice.

"I guess so," Lilly said, toying with the buttons on her lab jacket.

"Why do civilians have to clean up your messes?" demanded Chadwick.

"Lilly knows the answer to that question." A peculiar, tight expression crossed Garrison's face. "It has something to do with a homemade bomb."

"I promised someone my silence," Lilly said, her voice dropping to a whisper.

"You'd better reconsider your promise. Ordinary guns don't kill these things." Garrison's face got tighter still. It looked as if a fishbone had caught in her throat. "Eight people died in the woods this past week, including two of your neighbors. Six others evacuated their homes."

"Wade and I will hunt these creatures ourselves," Lilly told her.

"Then you're asking for trouble," Garrison said in a measured, quiet voice. "Homeland Security sighted another ship like the one that smashed through the woods behind your house. They suspect terrorists. Volunteer your information, Lilly, before I haul you to the station and confiscate your weapon."

"I knew this was getting out of hand." Lilly fanned her face with her left hand. "We'd better take this somewhere private." She waved Garrison toward the locker room. "The walls are pretty thick here. This should work."

Garrison stood against the door, arms folded, eyes meeting Lilly's squarely. "I'm listening."

Lilly sighed. "I'll level with you, but I need my weapon. These creatures remember, and they want me dead because I'm hiding a prisoner."

"Is this prisoner a survivor from the crash?" questioned Garrison.

Lilly nodded, her lips numb. "Yes, but he's not a terrorist. He lives on a planet called Eurosta. His people sentenced him to a death camp because he made a mistake. Those lizard-things – the Eurostans call them hydrii – guarded his cell and they survived the crash, too. His mistake was honest. His leader sent him to war, and —"

"You brought him to your home?" Garrison cut in with a fearful look. "You, your husband, and this visitor belong in quarantine."

"It's too late," Lilly said, more to herself than the officer. "I've spent the last four days doing patient care. So has my husband—but he works at Cherrydale Hospital."

"This poses another complication." Garrison sighed, exasperated. "We'll have to quarantine both hospitals."

"Quarantine?" Lilly gave her a gaped-mouth stare. "That's going to involve building new walls, negative pressure rooms, laboratories. ... oh, my God, Chadwick's not going to like it. Besides, if contact with these beings was going to infect me, don't you think I'd have symptoms by now?"

"I don't know. You might feel OK, but you and your husband may be carrying foreign bacteria from this other species. I can't have you risk infecting other people, especially patients." Garrison drew in a sharp breath. "I'm having a chat with your boss, and then I'll make some calls."

"Alright." Lilly followed Garrison to the hall, rubbing her temples, trying to stem a brewing headache. She stepped to the side as Garrison approached her boss. As the officer spoke, Chadwick's face turned several shades of purple. His mouth opened and closed without making a sound. A vein throbbed in his neck; his fists clenched and unclenched.

Garrison reached for her cellphone and went back into the locker room. Chadwick's eyes, burning with fury, fastened upon Lilly. "My God!" he shouted. "You have no idea how much damage this being or his people could do." He shook his head, clearing his throat. "Whatever possessed you to bring this being into your home?"

Lilly shook her head, fighting the tears that came to her eyes. "My mishap with Baby Miller. If it helps ..." Her voice quivered. "I've been wearing a gown, mask, and gloves around all my patients since I've been back on duty. Shouldn't that help contain the bacteria?"

"You don't even realize what you've done." Chadwick threw his hands in the air, then let them drop. "Those yellow gowns we have are useless," he continued in a strangled voice. "We'll need hazmat suits. Agent Garrison wants us in quarantine, no matter what."

Before Lilly could reply, Garrison stepped out to the hall again. "As we speak, two other agents are bringing your husband to Wyman Hospital, which handles unusual cases. Mr. Chadwick agrees that allowing you near patients would be unwise, so he found a replacement for you. Give him your report. When you're done, I'll drive you home so you can pack. Emergency Medical Services will arrive in about an hour or so to move you and your guest to Wyman Hospital, and I'll drive behind you in my van."

"I can drive to Wyman myself," Lilly offered.

"And perhaps take a detour so you can help

your friend skip out of town?" Garrison shook her head. "I'm sorry, but I'm doing this one by the book."

Chapter Eight
Trouble at Home

Lilly forced one leg before the other toward the chartroom where Muni waited to get her report. He moved aside a couple of charts that other staff using the room had left behind. Lilly nodded her thanks and managed a plastic smile, but inside, her heart hammered. After she finished giving report, she remained at the desk to collect her thoughts. Isolation, quarantine, the prospect of spreading an infection through the hospital—her mind slipped several cogs when she tried to grasp the enormity of it all. While she contemplated life in a hospital ward, a panicked scream blared through her head, slamming her against the chair back.

"LILLY, DON'T COME HOME! THERE'S GRAVE DANGER."

Lilly started panting and trembling uncontrollably. She blotted her forehead and took measured deep breaths. Her tremors eased. Another deep breath, and just when she felt ready to face the officer, the chartroom phone rang. It was Diane informing her that Garrison was waiting, to please hurry and wrap up her report. While Lilly flipped through her assignment sheets, making sure she'd hadn't omitted any information, her elbow brushed a chart, causing it to fall on the floor with a flat thump. Laylok's cry shivered through her mind again, and she gaped at the chart. Several pages had spilled out, and at the top one, the words LIVING WILL stared up at her in black spidery lines.

Oh, God, is it like that? She didn't know, but during the last few days, the thought of her or Wade dying had plagued her mind like a ...well ... like a premonition.

Death? For a moment, her life flashed before her eyes. She saw herself at school recess skipping rope. She recalled her high school prom with her then-boyfriend, not Wade. She relived her first dinner with Wade, where she had selected a Stuffed Chicken Marsala dinner at Olive Garden. Wade stood by her during her mother's death from leukemia. They laughed together and bought a house. They took turns driving her mother to chemotherapy treatments. He coddled her through Baby Miller's death and her illness, and now, their guest. Why risk her life for some stranger from outer space?

Because Laylok and I share a bond that even most relatives can't imagine. This bond came about because they each carry a radio inside their heads. Sometimes that radio, the telepathy, came in handy. At work, she could figure out a patient's symptoms, no matter what they failed to state. She knew which coworker might spread gossip to Chadwick. But sometimes she endured the bitter taste of pain, death, and danger. Laylok had gotten caught in that place, and she would do everything she could to help him. As far as she was concerned, that gift made her and Laylok siblings under the skin. If she ignored his cry and let him get killed, she'd never forgive herself.

But because she was human, she broke down into tears, clutching at her hair and whispering, "Why me?"

****

Two hydrii slithered from the bushes by her porch after Garrison's van pulled into the driveway. Lilly felt the reptiles coming, sensed them with her mind. She hopped from the van, weapon in hand. The hydrii cooperated by rushing at her. Lilly's shot bathed their heads in a sea of blue fire. Their hissing stopped. They collapsed, writhing on the grass, and then lay still.

"Not bad for someone wearing bifocals." She brayed nervous laughter. "Three dead today, plus others killed earlier. Fifteen more to go."

"Fifteen more what?" Garrison came up behind her, shouting through her hazmat suit.

"Hydrii." Lilly rubbed her arms, shivering. The cool wind nipped her cheeks as she and Garrison searched her yard. "Mind you, I can't do reconnaissance missions because of my vision, but my gift enables me to sense the approach of these creatures."

"What gift?" Garrison darted another glance through the yard. "Never mind, let's go in the house and find Laylok."

With an empty shrug, Lilly headed toward the porch. She jammed her key into the keyhole above her doorknob. Her fist went through air. Something had sheared the knob sideways, leaving a circular hole. "Look at that! They're chewing doorknobs now," she said, giving another harsh laugh. "There's another one for you, Agent Garrison."

With a deep sigh, Garrison furrowed her brows, her voice barely audible. "Then you'd better lower your voice. Is there another way into the house?"

"Yes." Lilly waved toward a brick building adjoining the house. "The garage has a door to the kitchen."

"Alright." Garrison's voice wavered; her body tensed. "Try not to make any sound and stay behind me."

They tiptoed across the yard, Garrison leading, gun at the ready. Lilly stayed close behind, clutching her beeper weapon, listening for the slipping sounds of hydrii. Right hand curled around her weapon and left gripping the knob, she cracked the door. No hydrii visible. Garrison moved on ahead of her; they crept in through the kitchen. Voices droned from the hall in a foreign language, one harsh, the other frightened. Although she didn't understand the words, the assailant's intentions played through her mind in the form of images.

She looked over at Garrison. Garrison held up one finger, making the quiet sign, and waved toward the hall. Her intent gaze reminded Lilly of a scientist studying a specimen, but the images in her mind warned that she anticipated shooting. In the hall, Lilly darted a glance inside the guestroom while reaching for her beeper device.

Laylok was already sitting up in bed, his face visible, blankets draped over his head and around his shoulders. The nasal prongs and concentrator continued feeding him oxygen. He was communicating by thought with his visitor, another Eurostan, who looked like he wanted to devour Laylok with his pointed teeth.

Mind-reading capabilities notwithstanding, Lilly had her health professional's ability to assess situations at a glance. The stranger wore a cement-gray suit that looked as if someone had assembled it from body parts. His head turned slightly, enabling her to make out part of his face. His glass shield revealed a mouth filled with sharp teeth and scarred cheeks, but his eyes spooked her. They were so red that to Lilly, they looked like pools of blood.

Laylok pulled off his oxygen tubing and stood up. *Lilly, run!* his mind pleaded.

I never run from a fight, Lilly thought back at him. Concentrating on the visitor, she saw him motion to Laylok. She couldn't understand his words, but the images came through. He was going to take Laylok to that death camp, without any blankets, oxygen, or other protection, and shoot any bystanders who got in the way.

Garrison nudged her shoulder and motioned toward the living room. After backing toward that room, Lilly and Garrison crouched behind a chair, their eyes facing the hallway. The stranger exited the bedroom, nudging Laylok with his weapon. He paused by the bathroom, looked inside, as if making an inspection, and then continued to the living room. When they got close, Laylok bent down to grab a blanket from the sofa. It gave both women a clean shot.

Reaching up over the chair, Garrison fired. The bullet shattered the stranger's face shield like it was fine crystal. The pieces fell to the floor in a wash of blood.

The stranger wailed in agony. His hands clutched at his face, but yellow pus and blood poured from his wounds like water from a burst hydrant. He staggered through the living room. Lilly hated what she was about to do, but she dared not let that get to her now. Ignoring the sound of Laylok's scurrying footsteps, she aimed her weapon. The laser whipped into the back of the intruder's neck, cracking bone. His shoulders exploded into flames, aided by the oxygen coming from his backpack. He took three shambling steps to the porch. Garrison sprinted out the door after him.

While the scene appeared as a fragmented swirl of colors and images, for Lilly, one thought remained: *I've got to make sure he's dead.*

Outside, the intruder collapsed headlong off the porch steps. His beeper gun dropped; it lay glinting in the sunlight. Garrison planted her boot-clad foot by the weapon and kicked it toward the bushes. The stranger lay flailing on the pavement. His hand, swathed in fire, moved toward Lilly. In a panic, she shot him again. Crackling followed as the laser burned through his suit.

The intruder stopped moving.

Lilly stood beside him, weeping out loud, her laser weapon dangling from one hand. Then she took two lurching steps, retrieved the attacker's sidearm, and vomited on the grass.

Garrison stepped up close beside her, her ruddy face glistening with perspiration. "I must say, for someone with poor vision, you demonstrated excellent marksmanship," she said, voice tinged with admiration.

"Thank you … I think." Lilly got up on weak knees and looked at Garrison. "Don't step on the puke."

Squatting beside Lilly, Garrison put her right arm around her shoulders. Lilly straightened slowly. "Talk to me," Garrison said gently. "Tell me about your guest."

"His name is Laylok and he's staying in the guest bedroom." With shaking fingers, Lilly pointed toward the house. "That other creep shut off his oxygen. He needs forty percent oxygen to survive. Without it, he'll die like Baby Miller."

Lilly swallowed hard.

"He told me this: His people – the Eurostans – sent him to a concentration camp—a death camp where people die of starvation—on trumped-up charges. The Eurostan ships travel in pairs on such missions. His ship went down, and someone from the twin ship came to follow up. This being was going to seize Laylok and kill both of us because we were in the way, so I was right behind you. I had no choice. I was acting in self-defense."

"You did what you had to." Garrison's voice softened. "We both did."

"I can't understand it." Lilly burst into strangled sobs. "I'm a respiratory therapist. I'm trained to save lives. No one trained me to kill."

"Even with training, it's horrible," Garrison agreed, "but you can get through it. You must because this creep probably summoned backup."

Garrison left Lilly and walked to the smoldering figure on the pavement. The intruder lay on his side with both arms obscuring his charred face. The shape of his melted plates suggested that both of their weapons had done some creative retooling of his anatomy.

"You handled the weapon like a pro." Garrison stood up and faced Lilly. "How?"

"Eurostan heat makes it easy." Lilly retrieved the assailant's firearm and handed it to Garrison. "Wade and I used weapons like this to kill the hydrii near our street."

"The what?"

"Hydrii – that's h-y-d-r-i-i – plural for hydrus. That's the Eurostan name for those lizard-things that killed your fellow officers. You hit the red button, and it shoots a laser."

"I was briefed on what happened," Garrison said, accepting the weapon. "You've still got that limp, so I'll report your injury to the Wyman doctors. Where's your suitcase?"

"Huh?" Lilly slumped her shoulders and gaped at the officer. *Now what?*

"Suitcase," Garrison repeated as they went into the house. "You know, the container for your tops, slacks, and things like that."

"Wade and I keep our suitcases in the basement. I should pack some clothes for him, too."

"I'll help you pack but first, I'd like to meet your guest. I also have a question. You've mentioned your gift and Baby Miller several times. Tell me about them."

They proceeded through the house in silence. The living room had a sour stench, but the hum of the oxygen concentrator and Laylok's voice inside Lilly's head assured her that he was OK.

She paused by the hall and let out a sigh. In a halting voice, she described Baby Miller's mishap, her surgery, and her encounter with Laylok, including the part about her telepathy. Images of a sickly woman streamed from the agent's mind at the description of Baby Miller's death. "The doctors came up with theories on how my telepathy happened," she finished quietly. "But really, they don't know."

Garrison arched her eyebrows. "Are you saying you can read minds?"

Lilly nodded. "For example, your mother has leukemia ... the same disease that took my mom ... and you were hoping to spend a weekend home with her. Instead ..." Something flashed across Garrison's face, a ghost of an expression—fear, perhaps. Whatever it was, Lilly shivered, her skin breaking out into goose bumps. "Instead, the Bureau mandated you to work."

Garrison drew in a deep breath. "What about

memories?"

"I can do distant memories," Lilly replied, eyes focused on Garrison, pulling images the way one might pluck flowers. "When you were twelve, your younger brother fell down the porch steps. He needed stitches on the top of his forehead. You were terrified because there was so much blood."

"Damn!" Garrison let out a low whistle. "You are good with this."

"Laylok and I communicate telepathically all the time." She paused outside the guestroom. "For your benefit, I'll announce myself verbally."

She tapped on the door. "Laylok," she called. "I brought in someone who wants to help. It's OK; she won't hurt you."

Don't do this, Lilly. No officers, please.

I have to, in case your attacker alerted his backup. Agent Garrison wants to help. I read her myself.

Laylok sat at the desk, wearing layers of wool blankets, nasal tubing in place. He was typing on a laptop, one letter at a time. The weight of the blankets slowed his effort. "Laylok needs forty percent oxygen and temperatures in the one hundred and fifty-degree range," Lilly told the agent. "When I found him, he was about to freeze to death, and his oxygen tank was running low. He reminded me of Baby Miller."

Garrison stared at Laylok, her eyes dilated from awe. "And so you brought this visitor to your home because you didn't want him to die like that baby did."

"That's right. I still have flashbacks about Baby Miller, and I don't want another pair of eyes following me."

"Agent Garrison understands," Laylok said. "Her mother is gravely ill."

Garrison turned toward Lilly, stiff-backed. "He just met me. How can he know about my mother?"

"Eurostans can read minds." Lilly nodded, confirming this to herself. "As can I."

"I need a radio to contact my home," Laylok said. "My telepathy can travel to the neighboring planets, but not far enough to reach my home. The radio I've made does not function."

"We can't ... we don't have the technology to build such a radio," Garrison said.

"This is unfortunate." Laylok's voice saddened. "The implanted tracking device we all wear enabled this soldier to find me. They'll keep coming around until I'm dead."

"Then you must realize it's no longer safe here," Garrison said, regarding Laylok steadily. "Our leaders offered to hide you, Lilly, and Wade. They can provide an environment that will meet your temperature and oxygen requirements, and they might try to find a way to disable this tracking device ... if this is possible. It will mean confinement, and you might ask yourself how important freedom is versus safety."

Laylok heaved a deep sigh. "Not only that. Your scientists will want to perform painful experiments."

"That's not true," Garrison assured him.

"People on Earth have never met beings from other worlds. Our doctors will run blood tests—presuming that you have blood—and x-rays so they can learn from you. Perhaps the outcome will enable them to find cures for cancer and other diseases."

Garrison lowered her eyes. "Perhaps what they learn can save my mother."

Lilly smiled, hoping to offer encouragement. "I think Laylok can make that happen for you."

"I don't want anyone to poke me for blood except Wade or Lilly," Laylok said.

"Are you good at taking blood?" Garrison asked, turning to Lilly.

"Wade and I collect arterial blood samples on the job. No complaints from any of our patients," Lilly replied, smiling.

"Consider yourself hired," Garrison said. "I'm surprised you were able to sense the hydrii ... even before I did."

"The little present my head injury left helped a lot," Lilly told her. "My mom once said that when a door closes, God opens a window. I think she had it right."

"Hopefully, this window will compensate for your vision problems that have made things difficult." Garrison put her hand on Lilly's shoulder and looked her in the eye. "You've earned the right to forgive yourself for Miller. Can you do that?"

"I'll try." Lilly nodded. "I appreciate ..." She turned, distracted by the roar of an overhead plane, followed by the jingling of a cellphone.

"It's mine." Garrison two-fingered her phone

from her pocket. She walked it into the kitchen.

"I still need to pack," Lilly told Laylok. "I'll get my suitcases. They're in the basement."

Moments later, she dragged two suitcases up the steps into the kitchen, where Garrison tucked her phone into her pocket. "Jerk!" she said in a low voice.

Uh, oh ... she had a fight with her boss. Lilly averted her eyes, not caring to let on that she'd read Garrison's thought. "I'm ready to pack. Emergency Medical Services should be here any moment, right?"

"There are two ambulances—it will take two because of all the isolation equipment involved. One's coming up your street. The other's been delayed in traffic." Garrison inhaled sharply. "My thought is that Laylok can go first, giving you time to finish packing."

Lilly managed a weak smile. "I appreciate that."

"Meantime, I have to investigate a disturbance in the woods. We've lost some of our key agents, so the Bureau has had to spread us thin." She sighed. "That means leaving you alone here, possibly until the Emergency Medical Services' second unit arrives. It's against the rules, and if you tried running ..."

"You'd get into a world of trouble." Lilly met her gaze levelly, her eyes resolute as steel. "Don't worry, I'm not going anywhere until the medics come for me."

****

Moments later, a van pulled to the curb. Four paramedics stepped out, all wearing yellow hazmat suits. Lilly recognized the insignia on their clothes and quickly led them to Laylok's room. They wheeled in a containment system—a hermetically-sealed plastic tent that would isolate Laylok from the medics and enable them to transport him to Wyman Hospital.

After saying her goodbyes to Laylok, Lilly rushed through her house, stuffing clothes, toiletries, and other items into two suitcases. She gulped down two cans of Ensure, leftovers from her hospital stay. She stood before a mirror, still in her work clothes, debating whether to shower, when she heard a blast outside. Chills inched up her neck, causing the hairs there to stiffen. The assailant's cavalry was coming. She knew this as well as she knew her own name.

The hell with Garrison's worries about the Bureau or contamination. I'll drive to Wyman myself.

With her suitcases in hand, she bolted to the door. Fear dominated; she badly wanted – needed – to escape. She put them down to haul open her door and screamed because an astronaut in a cement-gray, pressurized suit stood on her porch.

His red eyes looked out through a glass helmet. He brandished a laser beeper device. Suitcases forgotten, Lilly slammed the door and hurried to the kitchen. The door started opening, and another astronaut entered.

Lilly ran for a window. A sheet of metal

draped over it, and she watched in horror as two robots ... machines shaped like people ... soldered it to her window frame.

Moments later, another sheet of metal descended over the entire house. The house jittered and the lawn outside split open, resulting in widening cracks. The soil pulled apart in massive pie-shaped curves of grass. Roots strained upward below the green. Lilly ran toward another window and peered outside, watching the ground surrounding the house become bubbled-shaped, as if it were twisting to hold the house in place.

The foundation of the house cracked, and then crumbled. It ripped open with exploding mortar. Brilliant blue flames lanced out below the window. Screaming, Lilly covered her eyes and staggered to the sofa. Engines overhead blasted a deafening roar. The earth pulled up again ... and then let go. The house jerked about, rushing skyward, catapulting Lilly to the floor. *What a liftoff,* she thought, as waves of gray washed over her.

Chapter Nine
Lilly Takes a Trip

When Lilly opened her eyes, she lay sprawled on the floor. Her head throbbed as if someone had whacked her with a sledgehammer. A sickly sweet odor assaulted her nostrils. Her porcelain music boxes lay in shards amidst the scattered chairs and end tables. The sofa tipped forward, its arm inches from her outstretched hand. Her glasses had sailed to her left. They were poking out from under the radiator.

When she heard loud, whirring noises from above her, she felt through her pockets for her weapon. Empty. The floor slanted at about 30 degrees; the furniture had slid to her right. Bracing herself against a chair, she struggled to her feet and took two shambling steps. Her foot snagged on the telephone wire. She grabbed the chair to brace her fall.

Sharp angry words in a foreign tongue pierced her mind like icepicks. She tried to stand again, and the cord tugged on her injured leg. Cursing softly to herself, she grabbed the phone and flung it against a wall.

The throbbing worsened. Maybe someone had knocked her unconscious. Maybe she didn't want to know for sure. She opened the door and went into the bathroom, thinking she'd get some aspirin until it occurred to her that someone may have tainted the water. Perhaps the aspirin too, though she doubted that her kidnappers had taken the time to go through her medicine cabinet. But definitely the water. The thought gave her chills.

Passing back through the living room on her way to the kitchen, aspirin in hand, her lab coat flapping like a sail around her lean body, she shot a glance right and left. The kitchen table leaned against the wall's chipped tiles. Chairs lay on their sides. The cabinet doors hung open, having expelled their contents in a sea of shattered glassware on the countertop and floor. Ditto for the refrigerator, which tilted like the tower of Pisa.

Her gaze shifted toward the lunchmeats on the floor, still in their wrappers. She returned them to the refrigerator. Its steady hum assured her that for the moment, her perishables would remain fresh, and that somehow her house was getting electricity. She swallowed the aspirin with orange juice.

She went back to the living room and fished her glasses out from under the radiator. The lenses and frame appeared intact. She looked out her window. The sheet of metal was gone, replaced by what appeared to be a porthole. A metal door with a porthole and airlock replaced her wooden front door. The side porthole revealed the Earth, a maze of oceans and continents nested in the black, star-studded sky. She swallowed hard, her throat bone dry. Her fear turned from dread into terror that loomed large inside her; the yammering of her panic worse than it had been in the NICU, if possible. A a scream built up inside her throat, but she clamped her teeth against it, for if she were to let it out, it would exit as a bloodcurdling shriek.

I won't scream, she told herself fiercely. *I won't scream and provoke whoever's flying this thing to come out and sedate me, maybe worse.*

But now that radio in her head, the one that enabled her to tune into others' thoughts and memories, was picking up frightening undercurrents of something coming from the bedrooms. Rubbing her arms and shuddering, Lilly forced one foot before the other to her bedroom, aware, too aware, of how hard her heart pounded: *ka-boom, ka-thud. Ka-boom, ka-thud. Ka-boom, ka-thud.* She felt the beating in her ears. Her doctor had predicted that stress would one day kill her, but she refused to die in outer space. She needed an escape plan.

Then voices screeched something about Laylok and the hydrii, and the icepicks drilled through her head again.

She stood outside the bedroom until her gasping eased. Now she heard *ka-boom, ka-thud, ka-boom, ka-thud* again. The booming stopped. She imagined herself as a patient in an ICU, and then willed that picture away. At thirty-five, she was too young for a coronary.

She put one foot into the room, then thought

the better of it and remained at the doorway, listening to the rage in the voices. It reminded her of the fury she heard from Baby Miller's mother the day her baby died. If only she'd taken a job that didn't involve neonatal care. *If only.*

Harsh drilling noises rudely jerked her to the present. Fists clenched, she charged into her bedroom and screamed.

Two astronauts stood on her bed, their Eurostan features visible through glass shields. Surrounded by ceiling tiles that lay strewn across her bed and floor, they had cut holes into the sheetrock of the ceiling. The astronaut in cement gray was rerouting wires through one hole. His companion, dressed in black, was sealing pink glassy domes over the other holes with what she supposed was adhesive. Their lips never moved, but their animosity was evident.

"Hey!" Lilly shouted. "What are you doing?"

The astronaut in gray gave her a dispassionate look. "We're installing extra power lines to help maintain your electricity and gravity," he said.

"Power lines?" Lilly pressed her hand against her lips to keep them from trembling. Her mouth opened and closed, but no further words came out. Here she was alone in outer space with these hostile aliens, no pressurized suit or weapon. She swallowed hard, fighting back tears, her lips forming a widened O of horror.

"Our power lines are safer than yours." The astronaut in gray smiled, as if offering reassurance. "Humans use inferior sources of energy which can cause fires. Ours do not."

Lilly's eyes skated toward the ceiling again. She gasped, her voice trembling. "Why are you installing monitors?" she asked in a small voice.

"Because your house is now part of our ship," the man in gray told her. "We needed it to provided extra space for us to store equipment."

Another gasp. Her breath hitched. "Why ... why me? Why my house?"

"Because we hope to reach an agreement with your government. We have reason to believe that your officers are hiding Laylok, so we'll release you in exchange for him. The King doesn't want us to —"

"Be silent!" his partner ordered. "That goes for you, too, woman. We don't like people to ask questions."

"My name's Lilly," she stammered, cringing against a wall. "I'm asking questions because you destroyed my house."

Neither astronaut answered. They continued to work in silence.

Lilly sat on the floor to watch the Eurostans and probe their minds. Their words were unintelligible, but the images were vivid: The one in gray radiated brown and purple hues, along with images of him playing with two Eurostan children in a garden filled with blue shrubbery. She also saw an apparition of an older child who had died. She saw the astronaut in gray program a titanium robot while talking with an older Eurostan male wearing a gold robe.

Studying his companion, Lilly telepathically saw him admiring a room filled with marble statues. She watched him use his laser-gun on Eurostans tied in chains; she also heard him conversing with a group of men wearing blue, like football players in a huddle.

"What are you staring at?" the one in black snapped.

His intent stare made Lilly flinch. "Both of you," she replied, swallowing hard. "I never met Eurostan repairmen."

Hugging herself and shivering, she went back to the living room. She'd given the Eurostans a dumb answer but she'd rather that than then admit she was probing their minds. She righted the sofa. Except for tears in the fabric, it appeared intact. Taking a seat, she concentrated on Laylok. *Laylok, I'm in big trouble. Can you read me?*

She sat still, waiting for a thought to materialize, but none did. The despair that circled her, circling the way Laylok's ship did before the crash, weighed heavily on her shoulders. What made her think she could communicate by thought from outer space?

I'm on a Eurostan ship, Laylok. Can you read me?

Nothing. She yawned, fighting an onslaught of exhaustion, and glanced at her watch. Cracks splayed along its dial, and one hand had fallen to the side. Perhaps her watch shattered from the force of the liftoff. She checked the kitchen and bedroom clocks. Also broken. It didn't matter. *I've got to*

do something mundane to keep my head together.
Maybe eat something and clean up the mess.

Head stooped, she poked her way through
the broken dishes and glassware. Her fingers scis-
sored around a bag of pretzels. She ate three and
chased them with spring water. On she plodded,
scooping and heaving. Her mother-in-law's good
china. Drinking glasses. Jars of pickles and other
condiments. She worked her way to the kitchen
porthole, stopped, and found herself staring into
another room.

The porthole revealed the inside of her jail-
ers' ship.

In this room, two robots were working flashing buttons and dials on wall panels. No surprise
there. Not even a tiny one. From what Laylok had
told her, Eurostan technology ran centuries ahead
of Earth's. Each robot wore beeper devices at their
sides. The room teemed with hydrii, florid with red
plates. They crawled on the floor, the chairs, the
computers; one even climbed to a pink light fixture.
Their bulbous yellow eyes fixed on her. Their narrow black tongues flicked between rows of razor-
sharp teeth.

"They won't attack unless you try to escape,"
a voice said behind her.

Lilly whirled around and recoiled. The astronaut in gray stood by her table, hand clutching a
laser gun.

"Don't point that thing at me," Lilly said in a
low voice. "I'm harmless."

"The soldier you killed wouldn't agree," he

said, tucking his sidearm inside its holster. "My superior ordered us to watch you."

"I don't think I'm going anywhere in outer space," Lilly said in a dry voice. "How did you learn English?"

"Every astronaut learns English and other languages. Why don't you call me Taulir? Make it easy on both of us?"

Lilly drew in a deep breath and smelled stale oil. Laylok had that same scent when she first met him. *He smells like he sweats oil.*

Taulir gazed at her unblinkingly and chuckled. "In my opinion, humans display all different kinds of smells, but that is not my concern. I am worried about Laylok. The King judged him unfairly, don't you think? I wish I knew where he was so I could help him."

For a moment, Lilly was so startled by his expression of sympathy toward Laylok that she opened her mouth, about to tell him. Then she realized he was trying to trick the answer out of her. Instead, she remained quiet and imagined Laylok at a party shop, hugging and kissing a Mylar balloon.

Taulir laughed. "Playing with children's toys? I think not."

"Why should I tell you? You want to send him to some death camp."

"Either way, he'll die," Taulir replied without emotion. "Your atmosphere will poison him."

"That's what you think." Lilly met his gaze. "You're trying to trick me into giving you information. I can tell because I've worked with people for quite a few years."

"That's ridiculous!" Taulir burst into gales of laughter. "Don't even try to compare us to humans. What a joke."

A joke? She guessed that Eurostan technology made that of humans seem laughable. Ditto for telepathy; Taulir probably knew when she'd taken her first step. She trod back to the living room, bracing her hands against the walls in case the ship took a sudden lurch. Her chest felt heavy as stone. She looked through a porthole at the star-studded universe, then returned to the kitchen.

"I may not be the sharpest knife in the drawer, but I *can* read minds," she said at last, meeting Taulir's gaze.

"But you're a human, not an eating utensil."

"It's a figure of speech." Lilly sighed, her voice weary and slow. "You enjoy playing with children in a garden with blue plants, but you're thinking of another child. You build robots for a living. You also dislike your partner."

Taulir stood still, gazing at something on the wall. His lips didn't move, but his thought came through, in English: *Ivyr, come in here. It seems Laylok altered the cell chemistry in Lilly's brain.*

"Laylok didn't do anything to my brain," Lilly said aloud between clenched teeth.

Taulir's head swiveled toward Lilly. He gazed at her reflectively. "If you've had contact with Laylok, you know where he's hiding."

"Maybe I do," Lilly said, feeling an absurd sense of pride, "and maybe I don't want to tell you.

Your plans won't help Laylok."

Taulir's eyes twitched. Footsteps bounded from the hall, and then his partner Ivyr ran into the living room. His mind reached out and scanned hers, perhaps double-checking what Taulir knew and what Lilly had told him.

"I should feed you to the hydrii," Ivyr said, giving her a hard smile. "And I will after you see what I planned for your city. You deserve it for harboring a killer."

"If you hurt Lilly or any other human, Earth's officers will retaliate," Taulir told him.

"He's right," Lilly jumped in, emboldened by Taulir's defense. "Our so-called prehistoric methods employ sophisticated weapons and efficient soldiers."

"Efficient?" Ivyr snorted. "Don't make me laugh."

"Laylok shot the wrong man because your officers dressed him in the uniform of the enemy, Laylok mistook him for the enemy. You think that's funny?"

"We don't allow errors," Ivyr said. "Our society demands it."

"If that's true, then I thank God I'm human," Lilly told him.

Her captors did not answer. They had the advantage, and they knew it. But Lilly could take comfort in two things: Taulir and Ivyr didn't expect to meet a human telepath; and judging by their questions, neither man had detected Laylok's tracking device.

Lilly intended to make sure they didn't find out. At least not yet. Head lowered, she proceeded to her bedroom. She needed a shower, but she dared not with two strange aliens in her house and the threat of tainted water. She'd have to settle for a change of clothes. Sorting through her suitcase, she happened upon beat-up dungarees and a sweat-shirt, and underneath those she found a new silk top with sequins and matching slacks, a gift from Wade when she was in the hospital. Her eyes shift-ed between the new outfit and worn clothes. She sighed.

"Like Mom used to say, the President's not going to stop by today," she said, reaching for the dungarees.

Something metal gleamed underneath the clothing. It was Mark's watch. She'd forgotten that she'd packed it. This one still worked; according to its dial, it was 4:00 p.m. If it was accurate, she'd been in space about two hours. Heaving a deep sigh of relief, she pocketed the watch.

Ivyr's thoughts trailed her as she proceeded to the bathroom, and her mind saw images of him pouring vials of liquid into the pipes leading to her bathroom and kitchen.

Lilly tried the sink faucet, leaped back and screamed.

The water came full force, peeling off the enamel from the sink. The acid, or whatever it was, ate through the enamel, leaving bare metal. *Ivyr really intends to kill me. I bet later, he'll turn on Taulir and shoot him, too.* The hate bled through his thoughts in deep shades of crimson and black. Still screaming, she barreled to the kitchen, where Taulir and Ivyr stood like sentries by the other airlock. "You lowlifes!" she shouted. "Why did you poison my water?"

"You weary me," Ivyr said, pointing his gun at her head. "Give me one reason I shouldn't kill you."

Lilly's tongue stuck to the roof of her mouth. Her life depended on what she said to these Eurostans, and the words wouldn't come. She couldn't even loosen her tongue. *Why bother*? It was the voice of guilt, her old friend. *Why not let these men kill you? Consider it payback for Baby Miller.*

Because I've earned the right to be forgiven.

Taulir reached for his weapon. He lifted his face, revealing expressionless features. Water vapor formed on his backpack and heating unit, both of which he needed to tolerate Lilly's climate-controlled room. She toyed with the idea of turning her thermostat way down to freeze them but of course, the Eurostan heating units would protect them. And if anything happened to them, who would fly the ship?

Lilly tried to think, but her mind became a blank slate, the way a student's might during an intimidating examination. Her mouth opened in a black "O" of terror. *Taulir is going to allow Ivyr to do what he pleases.*

Instead, Taulir turned toward Ivyr. "Let her go," he said. "Lilly and I have unfinished business."

Ivyr looked at Taulir and laughed. "What business? She killed one of our own."

"Her government will retaliate if we harm

her," Taulir reiterated.

"Your family trouble has made you soft." Ivyr tucked his gun inside its holster. He withdrew a handheld device studded with buttons, and typed something into it. "I programmed my device to release a deadly gas through your air vents in one Earth hour. Escape, Lilly, and the hydrii will get you. Either way, you won't have an easy death. Taulir, you have one hour to finish your business." With that, Ivyr turned and exited the airlock.

"You knew about the tainted water," Taulir said to Lilly after the door shut behind Ivyr. "You really are a strong telepath."

Lilly's tongue finally became unstuck. "I tried to tell you." With calculated movements, Lilly went to the airlock and placed her hand on the lever. After Taulir did nothing but watch her without expression, she retrieved her hand and turned toward him. *Don't be ridiculous. It's not like he ignored you at some party.*

Once she did that, Taulir nodded and smiled, as if they *had* met at a party. "I doubt the concussion altered your brain cells. Perhaps your body carries aberrant DNA," he said, smiling. "Your healers wasted good money trying to understand your talent. They should have accepted it and moved onto another project."

"You didn't stop Ivyr because I knew he poisoned the water," she said. "You stopped him because I can describe your land: dome-shaped titanium structures surrounded by exotic blue flowers and a pink sky. Your leader insists on obedience.

He loves the color gold."

"Tell me something I don't know," Taulir said, still smiling.

"Ivyr plans to kill you."

"Wrong, Lilly," Taulir said. "The King considers me vital to this mission."

Trying to probe Taulir's mind, Lilly made out images of white smoke, which blocked out his thoughts. She tried to penetrate that barrier, but her head was aching again, making concentration difficult. Instead, she focused on Ivyr. His thoughts read like movie scenes, scenes of him shooting her and Taulir; images of him loading a gadget with flashing numbers on a small shuttle that was headed to Earth.

"Someone forgot to tell Ivyr that," she said after a pause. "Maybe he knows and doesn't care."

Taulir leaned against the wall, head down, and smile in place under his shield. Couldn't *he* mind-read Ivyr's plans? Lilly sensed that he did, but he refused to believe it. *Can I blame him?*

"Ivyr is sending a shuttle to Earth to bomb my city." She massaged her head, trying to ease the aching. "Probably several cities, and then *poof!* Radioactive fallout ... two million ... four million ..."

Taulir's smile dropped off his face, but the smokescreen guarding his mind remained intact.

"Ivyr made a deal with someone named Aurias ... or something like Aurias."

Taulir gave her a sharp look, but guarded his thoughts. Lilly kept reading Ivyr, despite her headache; according to her watch, she had forty minutes before the deadly gas was released. "My officers are hiding Laylok, and I did kill your soldier, so Aurias wants to teach us not to interfere. Do you know this woman?"

Lilly saw that he didn't. Around Taulir, Ivyr must have concealed his plans behind his own mental smokescreen. Taulir had never met anyone named Aurias. In addition to her headache, what felt like an iron band closed around her chest and squeezed. Was she having a heart attack? She prayed not.

"Ivyr sold information involving your King to these soldiers wearing blue uniforms. It wasn't the first time, either."

This earned Lilly a sudden crack in Taulir's mental wall. *Progress? Maybe.*

"According to Laylok, the *giestan* wear blue. These people pay Ivyr well for his trouble. After they assassinate your King, the *giestan* will overthrow your government. Your so-called superior telepathy didn't tell you that, did it?"

The throb in her chest deepened and sank into her heart like an axe. The room swam around her, forcing her to steady herself against the wall. She sank to her knees, weeping out loud, and saw Taulir heading toward the airlock. Not knowing what she was going to say, knowing that it was her last chance, she screamed, "The *giestan* shot your oldest son, and you never tried to stop them. You crumbled then like you're crumbing now, you coward!"

Chapter Ten
Chest Pain

Ahead of her, his back to her, Taulir stepped away from the airlock. He turned toward Lilly, who was sobbing, tears running down her reddened cheeks. The scabs on her leg had begun to itch.

"My son died five years ago," Taulir said. "Humans can't read distant memories."

"You know I'm an exception." Lilly struggled to her feet and dried her eyes. She hated delivering bad news to anyone, even Taulir. "Ivyr is your problem, not Laylok, me, or anyone else from Earth. Ivyr, your so-called partner, planned this litany of murders, and after me, you're his next hit."

"Why didn't I see this coming?" The whirling engines drowned out Taulir's soft voice, but Lilly read the words from his mind.

Taulir looked out the porthole in her kitchen. Lilly stood beside him, looking, and this time saw four robots lumbering back and forth, carrying metal crates with blinking lights. No people. Yet the room was mercilessly bright. Despite the roaring engines, the sounds of the buzzing alarms, static-like devices, and the barking of a commanding voice came through clearly. Someone was giving orders. Goose bumps popped up on her skin at the thought of what those crates with the blinking lights might be. Her teeth chattered.

"You are right. I never avenged my son's death," Taulir said. "I can set things right by stopping Ivyr and helping you escape. Do you have Laylok's pressurized suit?"

"He left it in my closet. It's got a broken temperature module and empty oxygen tanks."

"We carry spare parts for those modules, and I'm trained to fix them. We can share air until I get you a fresh tank. The short-term exposure to our oxygen concentrations won't harm you."

"Actually, I need the extra oxygen." Lilly gasped. "I ... I'm having trouble breathing."

"I can see that. You think something attacked your heart. My tissue analyzer could define your problem, and besides, the King would find the workings of human telepaths intriguing. Would you object to a blood test and microfilms of your anatomy?"

"Not at all, given the circumstances. Where will you do these tests?"

"At the laboratory near the life shuttles."

"Life shuttles?" Lilly's eyes widened.

"All ships have them. They offer more protection than one would have beaming to Earth. I'm surprised the crew on Laylok's ship didn't use them."

"I think the explosion surprised them." Lilly grimaced at the stabbing in her chest with each intake of breath and checked the time. "We've got less than thirty minutes for me to don that suit and you to fix the temperature module."

With Taulir's help, Lilly slipped Laylok's suit over her clothes. She tucked her wallet, which contained her photo ID, and aspirin into her holster. The holster clicked shut around her waist, and Taulir slid the helmet over her head. The suit fit, though she gagged on the stink of oil.

Taulir worked quickly, connecting the oxygen hoses, and threading and rethreading the wires to the heating module. After he replaced the microchips, he draped it over her shoulders and chest. The module hummed smoothly, cooling the gas flowing into Lilly's suit. The laboratory faced the far side of the ship, opposite the life-shuttles. It shone as brilliantly as the other Eurostan-built chambers on the vehicle. Something in Laylok's helmet enabled Lilly to detect smells, and with the oily odor came stomach churning followed by an impulse to vomit. She swallowed hard, fighting back the urge, trying hard to ignore the smell.

Using a device that allowed contact with skin through the suit, Taulir withdrew enough of Lilly's blood to fill a test tube. Lilly then walked through a chamber with flashing yellow lights, feeling sleepy despite the voices tumbling around in her head and the throbbing in her chest. She heard Taulir's footsteps before he spoke from outside the chamber.

"According to the analyzer, your hemoglobin is low on oxygen," he told her.

"How low is low?"

"Eighty-six percent," he replied. "The films show dried blood in the vessels of your right lung."

"Dried blood means a blood clot," Lilly said. "Lung clots and low oxygen are dangerous. The extra oxygen will help but I need blood thinners. Does your ship carry any human-friendly medications?"

"The analyzer calculates formulas for all medications, but I don't have the training to use them. Does this sickness kill?"

"It might, without treatment. I've got aspirin, which works like a blood thinner, but I can't take it without food."

"I can synthesize generic fare compatible with humans, but first I have a question. Lie to me, and I'll leave you here to die."

"OK."

"Why did you invite someone like Laylok to your home?"

"Why do you ask?" Lilly thought she was too out of breath to argue, but this seemed not to be the case. "You've got another agenda?"

"Just answer the question."

"Before my surgery, I cared for a sickly infant named Miller. Something I did messed up his ventilator, and caused him to die. Laylok was freezing to death when I found him. Watching him suffer was like watching Baby Miller die all over again." At that statement, Taulir let out a mournful sigh. Lilly winced at the sorrow piercing her heart when she read the fear in his thoughts. "Laylok taught me how to kill the hydrii that survived the crash. The ones on this ship frighten you, don't they?"

A glass slide dropped through Taulir's fingers, shattering on the grid floor. "The hydrii love the taste of blood. Species doesn't matter."

The machine to his left beeped, and its front panel opened. Reaching in, he retrieved a sack wrapped in metallic material. "Take this with your aspirin when we get on the life shuttle. Keep telling yourself that you're locked in the house so that Ivyr doesn't read your whereabouts."

"I hope this shuttle has spare oxygen and laser weapons," Lilly said.

After dropping his other slides into a compartment above the analyzer, Taulir walked her to a bell-shaped craft large enough to seat six adults. The inside was dark and smelled faintly of oil. Two robots sat at the cockpit controls. Lilly sat behind them, hands on her knees, while Taulir switched her empty oxygen tank for a full one. He then reached into an overhead recess filled with laser beeper devices and handed her four.

Moments later, metal bands slapped around Lilly and Taulir. They jumped at the deafening roar that followed, struggling to cover their ears but their helmets and the metal bands clamping down their arms made this impossible. The laboratory's lights disappeared, and in the next instant, Lilly found herself surrounded by an endless maze of star-studded sky. To their right, she made out the outline of the Big Dipper.

Ivyr's trying to scan your mind, came Taulir's unbidden thought. *Find a way to deceive him.*

I'm picturing myself in the laboratory getting

the blood test, Lilly thought back at him.

Good. I'll telegraph holographic images of both of us at the laboratory.

Are holographic images like virtual reality?

Yes. I'm hoping to distract Ivyr.

Lilly shifted, trying to ease her chest discomfort, but the vinyl-like seats offered scant padding. Her breath came out in gasps. The "meal," a paste she swallowed through a device in her mouthpiece, tasted like cardboard, but she forced it down with the aspirin. Though the shuttle blasted temperatures over 170 degrees F, according to a thermometer on the front panel, her suit radiated cool currents. Her eyelids grew heavy and she drifted to sleep.

A thump jarred Lilly awake after a long sleep. She sat before the open hatchway, facing the woods near where her house had been. "You dropped me so close to my address ..." she said to Taulir. "How did you do that?"

"I used the same coordinates I had when we landed here before." He pushed a button. The metal straps came loose. "The King judged Laylok too harshly. I know that now."

"Laylok wants to go home and clear his name," Lilly said, measuring her words with each breath. "You took great risks helping me, so maybe I should tell you his whereabouts."

"Ivyr's shuttle has left the ship with his timed bomb. If you even think about Laylok's hiding place, Ivyr will read you and target that spot. You can ask Laylok to warn your officers and find a healer to help you, but leave out any thought about his whereabouts. I'll stand watch."

"Laylok might know how to neutralize your bomb. If I summon him, he'll know where to find me. The officers can drive him and a doctor to Thorndale Street. I'm hoping that catching a traitor like Ivyr will earn you and Laylok points with your King. Meanwhile, find a way to distract Ivyr. I'll head to my street and shoot any hydrii along the way."

"Oh, Lilly!" Taulir sighed. "You have good intentions, but that clot, or whatever it is, could kill you."

"I'm aware of that." Lilly shuddered. "Let's pray it doesn't travel."

Lilly stared down the path, trembling, painfully aware that any telepath could read her, including Ivyr. After assuring herself that his attention was directed toward Taulir, she concentrated on Laylok. *I landed in the woods near your old ship. One of my guards, Taulir, brought me here.* Breath hitching, chest heaving in see-saw movements, she thought out each detail of her captivity at him. *Ivyr, the bad guy, is coming here with a bomb. Taulir's waiting for him. Can you dismantle a bomb?*

Yes, but I'm worried for you. You're in a lot of pain.

That's true. I've got a blood clot in my lung, and Taulir doesn't know how to treat it. Meet me at Thorndale Street with the officers, a doctor, and Wade. Tell Wade I love him.

While Lilly communicated with Laylok, rustling whispered from the trees to her left. Silence followed, long enough for her to conclude she was imagining things. Capital mistake. The clicks and slithering sounds came next. Gooseflesh broke out all over her body. The spit dried in her mouth.

Run, Lilly! Laylok screamed in her head.

Chapter Eleven
Two Specters of Death

I can't. She mouthed the words between pursed lips as she thought them.

Her shortness of breath made running impossible. Instead, she crept left, withdrawing her laser as she went. Adrenaline seeped into her blood. Selective perception fell away, and the hydrii's bright yellow eyes, glowing like headlights, illuminated every detail: the puddles of blood leading to Laylok's battered ship; a body clothed in rags; more hydrii slithering under the ship's dented hatchway. With fangs long as hairpins, the creatures reminded her of pictures she'd seen of dinosaurs. Underneath them, squirming in the blood-soaked grass, were dozens of baby hydrii. Coated with oily red slime, each stretched as long as an adult's forearm.

The adult hydrii rose up and hissed at her. Their tails lashed back and forth, and then lay over the babies to protect them. Lilly palmed her laser, aimed, and tracked the reptilian heads as they twisted and dodged. *Those creatures know what's coming.* She depressed the laser's button.

The blasts sang into the quiet night, and the hydrii disintegrated into balls of fire. The babies writhed and twisted, staring at Lilly with glittery eyes the size of marbles. If Lilly had breath to spare, she would have screamed.

Teeth chattering and breath rasping, she turned and walked on stiff legs with no feeling in them. She had no idea what she would do next until she spotted a pile of loose branches on the ground. With trembling arms and jerky movements, Lilly scooped up the branches and hugged them against her chest. She carried them back to the ship.

"I'm going to be your worst nightmare," she vowed, more confident now. She stepped toward the clutch of hydrii before the terrified sick person in her mind could seize the remote, turn her, and make her run. That person wouldn't care if her lack of oxygen killed her.

At least two dozen hydrii crawled under the hatchway. One raised its marble eyes toward Lilly and gave a hiss almost too high-pitched to be heard.

Still not allowing herself any pause, Lilly took slow steps toward the hatchway. A baby lizard skated across the grass toward her. She stepped on it; its body hadn't yet developed tough, protective plates. She tossed the branches before the hatchway. The hydrii skittered toward her.

Lilly stepped on another and saw that a third clung to the leg of her pressurized suit, holding on with its tiny claws, trying to bite through the material with its still-tiny fangs.

"Nightmare," she muttered, scraping it off

with the side of her other boot. Her face felt cold, yet it was drenched with sweat. Her breaths came fast, painful and shallow. If the hydrii didn't kill her, the blood clot could. She retrieved her laser again, but her hands shook badly. More of the plated reptiles crawled toward her. One wouldn't kill her, but an army might.

"Nightmare!" She depressed the laser's button, and it popped fire. For a second, the beam gave off a pink glow around the branches, and then ... *poof*! The branches became a nest of red flames. The flames spread toward the hatchway, blackening the branches. The fire reached the clutch of hydrii and consumed some of them. More hissing as the hydrii burned. Sizzling as their blood ran into the ground. Some of them darted under the ship.

Lilly backed toward the trees, shooting the laser as she went. More flames erupted, forming a red, gauzy curtain of smoke, giving the moon a reddish appearance. The heat baked against her face shield, fogging the glass. Chest pain gripped her. She imagined herself in the NICU again, trying to fix Baby Miller's ventilator. She saw him in cardiac arrest and shivered at his mother's accusations. An overwhelming urge to rush into the fire seized her.

Wait a minute, she thought. *Haven't I redeemed myself for Miller and earned my right to live?* "Nothing can bring you back, Baby Miller, and for that, I'm sorry," she said, weeping softly. "I mean it from the bottom of my heart." Then she turned away from the flames and shambled into the cold.

The wind and crackling flames drowned out

other sounds, but she heard panic-driven shouts. The wind blew sparks, igniting more branches. Darkness enshrouded the path leading to the street, and her telepathy did not compensate for her limited vision. She had to follow the sound of the voices and hope for the best.

Crunching footsteps came along moments later, and then Agent Garrison, Wade, and Laylok emerged from the brush. Laylok wore a pressurized suit. Wade had on his sport jacket. Garrison showed up in gray uniform. All of them carried guns.

"Lilly!" Wade folded her in his arms. "What happened to you?"

"The equipment on Taulir's shuttle says I have a clot in my lung."

"And you listened?" Wade shouted. "How could you believe anything those creeps say?"

"Two guards were holding me. One of them ...Taulir ... turned out to be a good guy. He helped me get here." Lilly paused to catch her breath. "Wade, I know what the symptoms are. I've seen them enough in my patients."

"She could be right," said Garrison. "What kind of tests did this alien do?"

"Taulir took a blood sample and did a scan of some kind—something like our CT scan. He gave me oxygen which bought me time. Even with the oxygen, though, it hurts to breathe."

"That did it." Garrison shook her head. "You're going to the hospital."

"Where's the ambulance?" Wade challenged her. "No one listened when Laylok requested a doctor."

"I wish you had sent a doctor." Lilly swallowed hard, fighting another onslaught of tears. "He could have given me something. But there's worse. Ivyr, my other guard, masterminded this whole operation ... used the house to store a bomb and other weapons to destroy Philadelphia and the surrounding counties. He's flying them here now. We must go to the landing site so Laylok can defuse the bomb."

"I know about this bomb," Laylok said. "Lilly relayed the information to me telepathically. She has the gift of telepathy, and it will lead us to Ivyr."

A smile crossed Garrison's face. "I've seen her gift in action."

"It all started with her mishap at the hospital," Wade said. "Something traumatized Lilly that made her receptive to other people's thoughts."

"Now that everyone understands that, can we start rolling?" Lilly pleaded.

"No way," Wade told her. "You've got no business playing *hero* with a blood clot."

"I had no choice when I stumbled on the hydrii nest near Laylok's crashed ship." Lilly hated the anger creeping in her voice, but her temper was running short along with her breath. "I burned most of them."

Garrison gazed toward the conflagration, eyes widened. "And that's what caused this fire."

"What would you have me do, Garrison?" Lilly sighed. "Run with chest pain and an oxygen saturation of eighty-six percent?"

"Of course not!" Garrison stepped back, her

face a shade paler. "You did what you needed to do to defend yourself; I understand that."

"With all due respect, Agent, I must neutralize that bomb before it's too late," Laylok said. "Lilly, take us to Taulir's shuttle."

"Lilly can't go anywhere," Wade snapped. "She's sick."

"We'll all die if Laylok can't get to that bomb." Garrison wiped her forehead and reached for her cellphone. "We can't leave Lilly here alone in her condition, and I doubt there's time to wait for an ambulance. Am I right, Laylok?"

Laylok nodded. "We've got to move fast."

"Right then." Garrison's eyes shifted toward Lilly. "How far is this other ship?"

"Not too far. Since all the trees look the same to me at night, Taulir can talk me and Laylok through the trek. He's waiting for Ivyr. I'm ready to go, but I've got to move slowly. Since my gift enables me to sense the presence of hydrii, I'll watch out for them."

"One more complication we don't need." Wade groaned. "When Ivyr makes his landing, stay to the rear and let us do the shooting. Let's go."

After focusing on Taulir's voice in her mind, Lilly followed Laylok, cutting between two oaks and up a narrow path where brush scraped her suit with its stiff bristles. To her right, the conflagration ate away the trees, but Taulir's thoughts guided her, as clear as if he'd used a microphone. She followed his directions with her head down, lips pursed, leading the others past the fire, over a bridge and around a curve, and then through a tangle of pines and oaks. Beyond that, a short footpath wound up the rise of meadow to Taulir's shuttle.

She stopped as fear struck her with corrosive force. Suppose Ivyr had already landed. What then? Shooting spree? Poison gas? An army of hydrii? Ivyr was capable of all those things and more.

Call the police.

Lilly giggled at that thought and leaned against a tree to catch her breath. She had, after all, brought a federal agent. In the movies, the cavalry would arrive, demanding Ivyr to surrender and hand over his weapons. Ivyr would raise his hands and stand before a firing squad manned by Laylok and she while the others watched.

It won't bring back Baby Miller.

Well, well. A tear trickled down her cheek, followed by another. Wade stood behind her, rubbing her shoulders. The hatchway slid open, followed by a mechanical hum. Taulir emerged into the clearing. Laylok gave her the "quiet" sign, then approached Taulir. The wind howled through the treetops. Lilly shivered.

She had no idea how long she knelt there, flanked by Wade and Garrison. The events happened so fast she was unsure of the time passing. Another shuttle landed, nested in blue fire. Its hatch unleashed a nest of hydrii, which took off toward the brush. Taulir fired at them, as did Lilly and her companions. The hydrii scattered and collapsed, consumed by flames.

Ivyr stepped forward, followed by three

armed robots. Taulir stooped, still watching for the hydrii, not knowing what was coming until it was too late. Ivyr's laser blazed him in the neck and head. The life-giving oxygen tanks became life-ending as the sparks ignited and consumed Taulir's body. The robots aimed their weapons and fired, drowning out the sound of his cries. Lilly ducked behind Taulir's shuttle seconds before a shot fired her way. Easing forward again, she shot at a robot. Her shot went wide and she missed hitting Ivyr's shuttle by inches.

Lasers stitched back and forth as the gunfire from Wade, Laylok, and Garrison shot down the robots. A shot singed Wade's arm, igniting his jacket. He calmly threw himself on the ground and rolled sideways to put out the flames.

Laylok approached Ivyr, stepping between the tongues of flames. He said something to Ivyr in Eurostan. Lilly sensed an offer to surrender if Ivyr would let the humans go. Laylok waved his hand toward Garrison, and she stepped over to Wade, to see how badly he was hurt.

Chest heaving, face dripping with sweat, Lilly studied Ivyr's mind. Understanding dawned, revealing his covert plan to shoot her, Wade, and Garrison. The images in his head came through clear as glass. Even now, he refused to take her telepathy seriously, and made no effort to hide his intentions. Her head swam and her surroundings blurred. The activity had used up more oxygen than her body could spare. "No," she whispered, "I can't faint. Not now."

She crept toward the clearing where Laylok and Ivyr continued their heated discussion, keeping her mind blank. Kneeling behind two shrubs, she pointed her gun toward Ivyr and fired. Her laser shattered his face shield. Another shot sent flames up his chest and shoulders. Howling, he took several lurching steps, and then collapsed. Laylok raced into Ivyr's shuttle.

Lilly shambled to the brush where Wade lay. His freckled face was pale as parchment. Spittle ran down his chin. His jacket sleeve sloughed away, revealing second and third degree burns. "I told you to stay back," he managed between grunts. "Why didn't you?"

"Baby Miller died because I followed the … the wrong orders." Her words came out choppy. Her lack of breath made it hard to finish her sentences. "Ivyr intended to kill us, and I'm not dying without a fight. Please … please tell me you won't either."

Gloved hands rested on her shoulders. Lilly whirled around and looked up at Laylok.

"I deactivated the bomb," he told her. "Ivyr used a simplistic device that I dismantled by cutting some wires."

"Thank you." Wade shifted and let out a cry. "Does your shuttle carry any painkillers?"

"Not the kind intended for humans," Laylok said gently. "Your healers can help, and both of you will recover. The Eurostan mind never prevails over the indomitable human spirit."

"You never know what you can do until you try." Lilly managed a lopsided smile. "Taulir did some tests on me, and he stored the results in his shuttle. He said my gift would impress your peers, so take that information to your King. Something there may prove Ivyr's treason and get you a pardon."

"I think it might." Laylok took Lilly's hands in his. "Thank you for your kindness. You too, Wade and Agent Garrison."

"You made this an interesting experience," Garrison said, grinning.

"I'll be thinking about you, Laylok," Lilly said. "Fly safely."

With that, Laylok stepped into Taulir's shuttle. The hatch closed, and moments later, the shuttle blasted skyward, trailing blue streaks of fire.

"We'd better blow this place before we fry," Wade said.

"How?" Lilly ventured a final look to her right. The fire still burned, though shrinking under the barrage of chemicals. "I've burned out our exit to Thorndale Street."

Wade, his ears perhaps catching the anxiety in Lilly's voice, struggled to a sitting position. "There's a trail on the opposite side of where those shuttles landed. Go around that curve and take the straight stretch. It will take you to Thorndale Street."

"Yeah?" Garrison looked at him with skepticism. "I'll call emergency medical services and see if they want to send a Medevac."

Lilly scanned the trees, but in the dark, they looked the same. No visible path. But she knew that Thorndale Street detoured around the woods and continued on the other side. Then her eyes settled on Garrison and her thoughts. "Oh, my ... Agent, a helicopter shouldn't be necessary. We can't be that far from the main road."

"We're about a mile," Wade told her.

"Can either of you walk that far?" asked Garrison.

"I can," Wade replied. "I don't know about Lilly."

"I've made it this far," Lilly pleaded for support. "I'll keep going."

With that, they trekked around the curve and toward the stretch. Wade groaned and clutched his arm, but he kept moving. A sharp pain knifed through Lilly's chest. She crumbled to her knees, gasping.

"Easy, Lilly," Garrison soothed her. "Take slow, easy breaths."

"Don't get up, honey," Wade pleaded. "You'll pass out if you keep going."

"If she hasn't done so already." Garrison looked down at Lilly, her eyes betraying alarm. "Lilly?"

"The pain's easing up, but my body feels like it weighs a ton." Lilly looked up at Garrison with exhausted eyes. "Wade's right about me. I'd better sit tight and let you call your emergency services. Think they'll be able to find us here?"

Garrison smiled. "I'll make sure they do."

Chapter Twelve
Months later

Another summer gone to seed. Lilly and Wade continued to visit the Wyman Hospital doctors who wanted to make sure that the Eurostans hadn't infected them. But Thanksgiving was coming, and all things considered, she found much for which to be grateful.

She was working a twelve-hour shift at Cherrydale Hospital, finishing her last ventilator check in the Intensive Care Unit. She and her former supervisor Diane had taken jobs there after brewing tension in Chadwick's department forced them to seek a healthier atmosphere. Her right leg healed with minimal scarring after the doctors repaired a torn muscle in her calf. Along with her lung clot, she had contracted pneumonia, both serious enough to demand a two-week stay in the hospital. The doctors theorized that the clot had formed in her leg and then traveled to the lung.

Winter had been her season to handle life-and-death problems … with mixed results.

Her patient, a woman, was doing poorly, face dark-tinged and glistening with sweat, and a thready pulse. While Lilly kept track of the monitors, her patient's pulse faded to a stop. The monitor alarm sounded, announcing a cardiac arrest, and Lilly was back in the NICU again, facing Baby Miller and his distraught mother. She hit the ventilator's "reset" button, but the whistling grew louder and louder.

And then NICU and Baby Miller faded, and she was working with Intensive Care's familiar machinery. *She's not Baby Miller* she reminded herself, regarding her patient with resolute eyes.

Lilly began chest compressions. Diane, who squeezed through the maze of uniformed professionals, fed oxygen through a plastic bag. The doctor on call shouted orders to the code team. Moments later, the heart monitor emitted rapid but steady beeps, and from the patient, Lilly sensed images of a husky man and a teenage boy kneeling together, hands folded, lips murmuring a prayer, and then the words floated like printed text:

I've got to live! My sick husband and son need me.

Lilly placed her patient back on the ventilator, ensuring she was now stable. Followed by Diane, she headed down the hall to the respiratory offices to give her report.

"Nice save," Diane said, smiling. "I bet you're happy that this one goes in your file."

"Thanks," Lilly said, smiling back. "Nightmares don't last forever."

"I know. You've taught me that."

"I think I like Cherrydale, and not just because Wade works here."

Behind Lilly, Wade's hand cradled her shoulder. He looked down at her and smiled. He had on a long-sleeved scrub shirt that concealed the scars on his right arm. She considered him lucky that the Wyman doctors were able to save his arm.

The government agents bought them a new furnished brick rancher closer to Cherrydale. Lilly would have settled for living in a trailer if it meant getting out of Wyman Hospital. The agents used a gentle approach; not an Ivyr or Chadwick in the bunch, but their questions brought forth horrible memories of the hydrii. They still attacked in her dreams.

"I've got your floor tonight," Wade said, heaving open the conference room door. "Anything interesting?"

"Code Blue in room 316." Lilly dumped her assignment sheets on the table. "Mary Billings, the one with emphysema and bilateral pneumonia. She made it, but she's got a tough recovery ahead of her."

"She's determined to fight," Diane said. "You probably know her story. I'm glad that you made it through everything OK."

"I'm grateful to be here ... and to be working with you." Lilly smiled. "Guess I'd better start report."

"And I've got paperwork to catch up on." Diane smiled and waved, then hurried to her office.

"She's right." Lilly turned toward Wade. "Diane figured out that I read people."

"It's hard not to notice," Wade said. "You knew we could trust Laylok and Taulir. You knew Ivyr was going to blow us away before he raised his gun."

"My mother once told me that when God closes a door, He opens a window," Lilly said. "Maybe He sent the telepathy to compensate for my poor vision."

"You could be right," Wade said. "We also learned something. We're not alone in the universe."

Lilly nodded. She and Garrison had become close friends, despite their surreal history. She went with Garrison to visit her mother, and later, the funeral. Visiting Garrison's mother was like being around her own mother, and that made a difference.

"Garrison assumed that people from outer space carried microbes lethal to humans," Wade said. "She had it wrong, and I think I convinced her of that. The Eurostans despise us, but that didn't mean they carry hostile microbes."

"Laylok considered us his friends."

"Taulir and Ivyr wanted bloodshed. They stole our home and memories."

"We lost a lot of family heirlooms, too; but Taulir apologized and made up for it," Lilly said. "He was a good guy, but we didn't know it at first."

They fell quiet. Lilly glanced at their coworkers, who were engaged in lively conversation.

"Your telepathy impressed him," Wade said,

regarding her with fascination. "The Eurostans didn't know what to make of it. I'll never understand how you managed the walk through the woods. If you hadn't gotten away ..."

"But I did get away. Taulir wrecked our house, but he saved my life. He took my films and blood tests..."

"Don't talk about those." Wade groaned, covering his eyes, and Lilly saw his anger. *He despised the Eurostans and considered Laylok's visit a disaster After all, it had nearly cost us our lives.*

"I'm sorry."

Wade waved his hand to show it was OK, but his face paled considerably. "Maybe those people were drawn to you the way flowers are to the sun. I can't be sure because they think so differently than we do."

"You think they'll come back?"

"I believe they will."

Lilly looked out the window. Already, the moon had risen, and an ambulance wailed in the distance. "When their king gets Laylok's report, they'll have a discussion, and then someone will send a mission to Earth for further investigation. But not this week." She sighed. "I guess I'd better give you my report."

Wade took Lilly's hand in his. Their eyes met, and Lilly saw his love. She smiled at him. He smiled back. Then they sat, and at the moment, the only darkness came from the moonlit sky outside.

About the Contributors

Barbara Custer: Barbara lives near Philadelphia, Pennsylvania, where she works full time as a respiratory therapist. When she's not working with her patients, she's enjoying a fright flick or working on horror and science fiction tales. Her short stories have appeared in numerous small press magazines. She's published *Night to Dawn* magazine since 2004.

Other books by Barbara include *Close Liaisons, Life Raft: Earth, Twilight Healer, City of Brotherly Death,* and *Steel Rose.* She's also coauthored *Alien Worlds* and *Starship Invasions* (both now out of print) with Tom Johnson. She enjoys bringing her medical background to the printed page and blending it with supernatural horror. She maintains a presence on Facebook, Linkedin, Twitter, and The Writers Coffeehouse forum. Look for the photos with the Mylar balloons and you'll find her.

To contact Barbara, e-mail her at barbaracuster@hotmail.com.

Visit her at: www.bloodredshadow.com
www.facebook.com/barbara.custer
https://twitter.com/NighttoDawn1

Marge Simon: Marge Simon's works appear in publications such as *DailySF Magazine, Pedestal,* and *Dreams & Nightmares.* She edits a column for the HWA Newsletter, "Blood & Spades: Poets of the Dark Side," and serves as Chair of the Board of Trustees. She won the Strange Horizons Readers Choice Award, 2010, and the SFPA's Dwarf Stars Award, 2012. She has won three Bram Stoker Awards ® for Superior Work in Poetry, two first place Rhysling Awards and the Grand Master Award from the SF Poetry Association, 2015. In addition to her poetry, she has published two prose collections: *Christina's World,* Sam's Dot Publications, 2008 and *Like Birds in the Rain,* Sam's Dot, 2007. Her poems appear in Qualia Nous (Written Backwards), The Dark Phantastique (Jasunni Productions), Spectral Realms anthologies by S.T. Joshi, and more poems will appear in Chiral Mad 3 and Scary Out There, a HWA/ Simon & Schuster Y/A collection, 2015. www.margesimon.com